Shanghai Torah

Yuanfen

Briana London

www.shanghaitorah.com

COSWORTH PUBLISHING
21545 Yucatan Avenue
Woodland Hills, CA 91364
www.cosworthpublishing.com

ISBN: 978-1-970022-44-5

Jacket design by Charlie Sitzer

Dedication

In memory of my mother, Suzann C. Spears

Yuanfen: (Chinese)

The destiny or fate that brings two people together in an unlikely relationship.

Author's Note

One day my phone rang.

"Get your butt to the Temple. You never had a *bat mitzvah,* and I'm teaching a class."

I heard the voice, the one you trust, the one you never question. Frannie Morris Rosman has been my dear friend since we were eleven years old, and my faith in our friendship never wavered—until this phone call.

It was true that my parents happily nested in the comfortable stereotypes for raising girls and boys. Dictated by the 1950's, my brother was encouraged to play baseball, soccer, basketball; and for me, horseback riding and swim team. Our future careers—for my brother, medicine or law—and for me, marry a lawyer.

For my brother, a *bar mitzvah* was not a choice but a requirement. I was then forty-something and had a husband, a son, two dogs, and a horse. To top it off, I was working twelve-hour days editing television shows. I was so tired that I could hardly converse in my native language, so the idea that I would need to learn a new language seemed ridiculous and impossible. However, like I said, Frannie doesn't take no for an answer.

A few days later I was sitting in a class of forty adults. I wondered why they were all here and did they all know Frannie? There was a well-known recording artist, a retired aerospace engineer, a young publicist, and four converts amongst the group. I remember thinking—why would anyone want to convert to a religion that is so hated throughout the rest of the world?

I decided that I wouldn't fight the learning, though I doubted this experience would amount to anything more than a waste of my valuable time. Then, the Cantor, Nathan Lam, brought out the little Shanghai Torah.

The forty of us stood in a circle and held the parchment as Rabbi Ron Stern and Cantor Lam unfurled the scroll, recounting the story of how the little Torah came to Steven S. Wise Temple in Los Angeles.

I was stunned by the beauty of the penmanship; tiny and precise strokes made up each character imprinted upon the page. I was mesmerized by the idea of saving this little scroll from the terror of a Nazi assault on the Synagogue in Vilna. I was holding a part of what was once wrapped around the waist of a brave soul fleeing for his life.

Thinking about the original owner of this little scroll gave me chills. I thought a lot about this young man and his journey. Who did he meet? What about the differences in language and cultures? Also, who helped him during his times of struggle? How did he survive and then make it from Vilna, Lithuania, to Shanghai, China? What happened after the war?

So began my journey, the one in my imagination. I thought of his situation of being a fish out of water in a foreign land. I thought about the need for love during times of great oppression. I thought about the little Torah, its importance being so great that a young man would put it ahead of his own existence.

Finally, my experience learning a new language and discussing the stories of my ancestors reminded me of the vital and fragile relationship between the written word and our preservation.

Briana London

Introduction

The Recipe

How to be an ink chef:

Boil one pint of water.
Add ½ pint of (crushed) gallnut powder.
Add ¼ pint of (crushed) gum Arabic crystals.
Add 1/8 pint of (crushed) copper sulfate crystals.
Add 1/8 pint of (crushed) fine black carbon powder.

Mix together and store in a clean glass jar.

How to whittle a pen:

Find a quill from a turkey or goose. Using a scalpel or razor
blade, sculpt the stem of the quill into a fine point.

How to make the parchment:

Use the skin of a kosher animal. (It is very important that the
animal either died of natural causes or was killed for food).
Soak the hide in limewater from nine to eighteen days to soften.
Scrape hide to remove fat and hairs.
Dry hide on a stretching rack.
While on rack, sand and scrape until parchment becomes
smooth and flat.

To keep the letters straight and even, use a straight edge and
draw forty-three horizontal lines across the parchment. Make
three columns per page. Leave a blank margin four inches on
the bottom, three inches on the top, and two inches between the
columns.

After the ritual prayers, the washing of hands, or the visit to the
mikvah—the ritual baths—you are ready to begin.

On a scrap of parchment, write the name *Amalek,* Israel's enemy. Cross it out to erase the memory of a cruel ancient people who killed and maimed many young children, mothers, and Israelis.

Dip the quill into the ink and write: תישארב—*Bereshit*—In the beginning—the first word of a long and fierce story that binds one generation to the next; words that blend together to teach the laws necessary for the existence of a civilized society. Stories filled with the tug of war between good and evil, love, passion, greed, and rebellion. Words that shine like mirrors reflecting our human nature, presenting us with life choices and recipes for peace.

Bereshit—our journey begins.

Part One
Vilna, Lithuania 1939

Chapter One

A burst of cigar smoke punches Akiva in the face. He recoils. Nose to nose, blubbery blob pressed to button, Mr. Bernstein, the village postal master, utters an amazing proclamation—his words a soupy mixture of Yiddish and Polish.

"You are now twelve years old, Akiva. I make you the responsible one, not like your *meshuge* brother, Levi. Go now, take this letter to your big brother Moshe." Pulling the boy closer he whispers, "It's from America."

Akiva bolts out the door of the post office. His long, curly *payot* slap his ears as he runs past the stores facing the main street. With one eye guarding the envelope that is stuffed tightly in his small, pudgy hand, Akiva knows he has been tasked with an important mission.

Why else had Mr. Bernstein walked all the way around his desk to hand him the envelope personally? The old man never leaves his chair—ever.

Dusk to dawn Mr. Bernstein takes his naps and studies Torah until his wife Rachel brings in his meals. Akiva and his siblings are convinced that throughout the years Mr. Bernstein's rear-end has grown so large that one day he will be found deceased, stuffed into the seat of that creaky old chair. Then, he and the chair will have to be buried together. But, maybe that will happen in the near future.

Today, Mr. Bernstein had stood up sliding the chair aside; wheels smashing against the wall. He had bounded around the large oak desk and issued an order!

This has to be an important letter.

****

Mid-afternoon on a Friday means people are hurrying to wrap-up their errands. Sundown will herald the Sabbath, and families will soon join together to eat, pray, and rest. Akiva needs more fuel in his skinny legs if he is going to race the sun.

"Akiva! Where's the fire!" yells Mr. Penkowski as Akiva crashes into the open arms of the loud, jovial man with fish blood staining his dirty apron. Even worse than standing next to Mr. Penkowski is being hugged by him. Mama says that it takes four washings to get one of Mr. Penkowski's hugs out of clothing. Akiva jumps backwards.

"Sorry, I can't stop. I have an important letter to deliver!"

"Really? A letter? Let me see," he demands.

Akiva holds out the crumpled envelope, but instead of taking the letter, Mr. Penkowski shoves Akiva behind his large body. Two Soviet soldiers come to a halt.

"Ah, good afternoon officers," Mr. Penkowski says and gestures towards the row of fish lying on beds of ice. "The sturgeon is fresh today. So fresh it will slide down your throats and swim in your stomachs."

Peering around the big man, Akiva smiles at his reflection in the soldier's tall, shiny boot. The sun glints off the brass buckles that hook onto the leather. Akiva sticks out his tongue and laughs, but the boot returns an angry stomp onto the ground. Akiva recoils behind the fish man, who tightens his hold on the boy.

The soldier points to a large sturgeon glistening in the sunlight. Mr. Penkowski wraps the fish in a sheet of newspaper and hands the package to the soldier.

4

The soldier studies the patch sewn onto Mr. Penkowski's shirtsleeve; the embroidered yellow Star of David glares back. The soldier straightens, folds the wrapped fish under his arm, and says goodbye—no money is exchanged. When they are out of sight, Mr. Penkowski turns to face the boy.

"Eh! That was one of my best catches. I hope it bites him on the way down to his stomach. Pftt."

"Did he steal the fish, Mr. Penkowski?"

"No, *boychick*, it was a gift, and in return they will protect my shop when the Germans come. Go on now, the sun is setting and the Sabbath is coming."

Akiva slides the letter into the waistband of his pants.

"Go. Go. *Shabbat Shalom*. My best to your father, the *Rebbe*." Mr. Penkowski steps aside.

The young boy swings his right leg forward, followed by his left, and picks up speed. Two blocks down the street, Akiva cuts the corner short and smacks into Tanta Sophie. Looking older than her late thirties, she wears the mantle of *yenta* proudly.

"Slow down. What's the rush? You have a bus to catch?" she frowns. "Look, you made me drop my *challah*."

"Sorry," Akiva says, scooping up the loaf of bread. "I can't stop!"

"You don't have a moment to give a hug to your *tanta*?"

"Nope, I have an important job to do."

"What kind of job is so important for a twelve-year-old that he has to make his *tanta* drop her groceries?"

Akiva frowns; he doesn't like being scolded, especially by Tanta Sophie—whose face resembles a pickle.

Then he brightens. "I have a letter from Levi!"

"Ahh, from Levi. Where? Where is this letter?"

Akiva gathers up his *tallit katan,* exposing the envelope tucked into his waistband.

Sophie examines the letter.

"Well, this will be a good *Shabbat*," she smiles, "news from America!"

****

5

In the flicker of candlelight, Moshe hunches over a small piece of parchment. He keeps his mind focused on the task at hand, writing the words that hold sacred the history of his people.

A delicate balance exists between the amount of ink on the end of the quill and the pressure of his hand resting on the paper. A *sofer* must be careful not to let the oils from his hand smudge the ink. One mistake and he will have to start over. Several partially started sheets of parchment lie crumpled on the floor at his feet.

Coating this small attic room, mounds of dust belie the sanctity within. The room is small, cramped, and filled with stacks of parchment, old inkbottles, and quills. A golden hue of light licks the surface of the silver crowns that adorn the tops of several Torahs awaiting attention.

Writing a Torah may take a lifetime, and repairing tears and smudges may take two. Moshe looks up and draws in a breath of stale air. He enjoys the solitude of the work; the smells of the dusty old scrolls lining the walls, a sanctuary within a palace—*The Great Synagogue of Vilna*.

Inside his little attic studio, no fear exists, no Soviets, no Germans, only the words of God and a seventeen-year-old with a feather quill.

Since his *bar mitzvah* at age thirteen, he has imagined writing a single scroll, beginning to end—79,976 words comprised of 304,805 letters. It could take his entire lifetime to finish, and for that he feels honored.

Moshe closes his eyes and whispers a prayer. "I am hereby writing this *Sofer Torah* for the purpose of proclaiming the sanctity of the *Sofer Torah.*"

Then, when the moment arrives, his hand applies a steady pressure and the ink flows.

****

It has been said that Napoleon stood at the entrance of the Great Synagogue of Vilna and was rendered speechless. In fact, due to building regulations, the synagogue was built with two levels going below ground and three stories rising above. Though plain and unobtrusive on the outside, the interior is magnificent.

Designed in the Italian Renaissance-Baroque style, the cavernous main hall includes large marble columns, ornamental carved wooden detailing, iron balustrades, and bronze and silver chandeliers. The prayer hall can accommodate three hundred people. In the center of the room, four statuesque columns encircle the *bema*. Seemingly in motion, two stories tall, the columns swirl and curve with imposing, dynamic opulence. The rococo styled podium sits atop a stone pile three tiers above floor level. Overhead, the grand, ornately carved cupola directs a column of warm light upon the *bema*.

To Akiva, the synagogue is both wondrous and terrifying. Standing in the portal at the western side of the building, he throws all his weight against the massive iron door. It shifts a few inches. If he expels all the air in his lungs he will be able to squeeze his body through the small opening. Once inside, Akiva shrinks behind a massive marble column.

The synagogue is quiet now, but on *Shabbat*, and especially on the holidays, the room doesn't appear to be so cavernous. Those are the times when hundreds of voices chant, sing, and collectively raise a joyous spirit that wraps Akiva in warmth and love. Now, peering around, he gazes at the ornate ark standing two stories high along the eastern wall.

The ark is resplendent with carvings of Jewish symbols, animals, and plants, but it is what sits on the top that makes Akiva shudder. Perched high atop the ark doors is a carving of a two-headed eagle, daring all who approach.

Akiva has debated the significance of this bird with his friends. Is it a symbol of protection, warding against evil that might try to destroy the sacred scrolls housed within? Or is it, as his friend Dovid believes, a monster meant to scare away anyone who isn't *shomer Shabbos*. Whatever the reason for its existence, Akiva finds the eagle threatening and makes a point of hastening his steps whenever he ventures near the ark.

The crunch of the letter in his waistband reminds him of his task. Releasing his hold on the marble column, he moves away from the two-headed eagle, passes the stairway leading to one of the women's sections, and enters the library on the southern side of the building.

At the far end of the room a narrow stairway leads to Moshe's studio. Akiva follows a stream of sunbeams rising up the stairs. The light settles onto Akiva's worn out shoe as he lingers in the doorway. One step into the room, he will break the beam and complete his mission.

"Ah, Akiva, have you come to tell me that it is almost *Shabbos*?" Moshe asks without looking up from his parchment.

"Moshe, is that the Baby?" Akiva asks, pointing to a little Torah lying open on Moshe's writing desk.

Moshe smiles. "Indeed it is, and it is just your size. One day I will see you dance with this little one on *Simchat Torah*." He studies the wet ink. "Come, you can help write the final letter of the day."

Akiva climbs onto Moshe's lap.

"Okay, cover your hand over mine. Good. Now we will make a *mem*. See, it takes five strokes to make this letter. Each one is for the Five Books of Moses."

"I think the *mem* looks like an elephant with his trunk in the air. Do you see animals when you write your letters, Moshe?"

"I do, and I also see God." Moshe smiles, puts down his quill, and blows softly on the parchment.

"Make me an airplane, Moshe."

"Okay, get me a sheet off the floor and I'll teach you how to fold one."

Akiva selects one piece of parchment and hands it to his older brother. Moshe carefully folds the paper lengthwise in half, and then folds each side into two triangles making the wings. Akiva eagerly copies him, matching Moshe's paper airplane with his own.

"I hope that one day, Moshe, I will fly in a real plane and it won't be made of paper."

"I bet you will."

"Yep, and I'm going to ask the pilot to teach me to fly the plane."

"Where will you fly to?"

"I'll wait until Mama is cooking in the kitchen, and then I'll buzz over our house a bunch of times," Akiva laughs.

"Ha, that will make her mad," Moshe smiles.

"Yep, and she'll run outside and shake her fist at the sky! And you will know it's me, Moshe, because I'll tip my wings to say hello."

"I will look forward to your first solo flight, Akiva. Here's your plane. Let's have a contest and see who is the better pilot."

Moshe opens the window. "Go on, you can take off first."

"I'm going to try to land on the roof across the road," Akiva says and winds back his throwing arm, launching the plane with great force. It sails high above the street, hovering over the people chatting below. Midflight, Akiva's plane stalls, spirals, and lands nose down, piercing an apple on Mr. Pinkus' fruit cart.

"Uh oh," says Akiva, ducking below the windowsill.

"*Ahhhh!!*" Mr. Pinkus yells, shaking his fist at the window. "You rotten kids! I will make your mothers buy my entire cart!"

"Mr. Pinkus is really mad, Moshe."

"It's okay, his apples are mushy anyway," Moshe winks. "Okay, it's time for us to go. We'll have to resume our contest another time."

Moshe slips his paper airplane into the pocket of his wool coat and rechecks the ink on the section of the little Torah. "It looks like the ink is dry, so let's put the Baby to bed."

Akiva retrieves the blue velvet *mantel* while Moshe rolls up the little Torah and secures it with a linen sash. Akiva gently slips the cover over the top of the wooden shafts and carries the sleeping baby to a small wooden box leaning against the corner of the room. He gives the Torah a kiss and lays it gently into the little ark.

Moshe locks the attic door and Akiva follows him down the narrow stairway. The excitement of writing a letter in the little Torah and the airplane contest was a distraction. Akiva forgot about his promise to Mr. Penkowki—to deliver the letter from America.

Chapter Two

Rivka pulls her shawl over her head; her hands draw circles above the flames of the *Shabbos* candles. Her neighbor, Miriam Holtzman, along with her two teenage daughters, Elana and Sarah, join Rivka's three young daughters at her side.

Rivka covers her eyes and begins the chant that heralds the start of the next twenty-four hours.

"Baruch ata Adonai elohenu melech ha-olam," Rivka recites.

Moshe and Akiva stand in the doorway. Elana catches a glimpse and turns away. When she turns back, Moshe has one eyebrow raised and his lips scrunched.

Elana flares her nostrils in and out. Moshe makes fish lips. Akiva enjoys this game.

Rivka continues, *"Asher kid'shanu b'mitzvotav v'tzivanu l'hadlik ner shel Shabbat."*

The girls utter, "Amen."

Moshe crosses his eyes and Akiva bursts out laughing. Rivka throws a disapproving look to the boys. She turns to the girls. "May the Sabbath light forever shine in your lives and keep you safe in your homes," Rivka says, turning to Elana and Sarah, "and may this light shine your way to the arms of your future husbands."

Elana and Moshe smile at each other. Their friendship has endured since childhood. The families have integrated to the point where the mothers, Rivka and Miriam, are interchangeable. Moshe has always been like a brother to Elana. That is, until earlier this year. Racing through the woods playing pirates, she inexplicably took his breath away. Elana is no longer the little girl who could run faster or hit harder. Her once chunky body has grown soft and shapely.

He is keenly aware of how her brown eyes smile whenever she sees him; how her long, untamed curly hair collects leaves, twigs, and bugs whenever they walk in the woods near their homes. In reality, he has loved her since he was six years old, and it is his greatest desire that next year when they turn eighteen, she will become his wife.

"Girls," says Rivka, "come with me to the kitchen. Elana, you and Moshe bring in some wood for the fire. Be quick, the sun is setting."

Elana follows Moshe through the foyer towards the back of the house. They pause outside the door leading to his father's study. Inside, several men from the village and a couple of older students from the *yeshiva* huddle around the Rabbi's desk studying a large map. They speak in hushed tones, unaware that they are being observed.

As a little boy, Moshe would pretend that his father was born without eyes so there would be a good excuse for being ignored. People from the *shtetl* would wait for hours in the foyer just to have a quick moment to tell him their troubles. The Rabbi would sit with eyes closed, stroking his frizzy long beard and swaying before speaking. Whatever he said brought the women tears of joy and the men heaving sighs of relief.

Waiting in the doorway to his father's study, little Moshe hoped for a chance to sit in front of the Great *Rebbe,* his father, and hear his words of wisdom. Time after time, without even looking in Moshe's direction, the Rabbi would wave him away. There was one day when Moshe and his older brother Levi hatched a plan to get their father's attention.

This is how it would happen: drag a mattress outside to the backyard and position it underneath their father's study window. Borrow mama's heirloom quilt to use for a parachute, climb up onto the roof, jump, and land safely on top of the mattress. Papa would cease his studies as their bodies flew by. Leaning out of the window, looking down in amazement, Papa would marvel at his sons' ingenuity.

Here is how it went: dragged the mattress outside to the backyard and positioned it underneath their father's study window, covering mama's newly planted flowerbed; pulled mama's heirloom quilt along the ground, tearing the fringe off the bottom; climbed up onto the roof and jumped.

The howls from Levi after missing the mattress brought Mama running outside, screaming. First, she screamed about her quilt, and then she screamed about her destroyed flowerbed and, finally, she screamed at her naughty sons.

Levi and Moshe laughed and looked up to see a young *yeshiva* student poke his head out the window, glare down at the boys, shut the glass panes, and snap the drapes closed.

Levi spent the next eight weeks using wooden crutches to get around the house and the neighborhood. That first night his foot swelled to the size of a melon. Mama iced Levi's foot every two hours. Their father never came upstairs into their bedroom to visit.

The day of the "accident" was the beginning of a change for Levi. Always a bit restless, he preferred to wander into the back woods than to sit in father's study with the books. He also harbored bitterness deep inside. Like Moshe, he yearned for his father's attention, but he was born with the heart of a rebel—resisting authority—and Rabbi Lozinsky couldn't relate to his eldest son.

"Books are boring," he would tell Moshe. "One day I will travel to places where there are wonderful things to see, mountains, deserts, oceans, instead of reading about them on paper."

"But there are wonderful adventures in the Torah, Levi."

"Those are made up stories, Moshe."

"Maybe, maybe not. But how would you have known that there are wonderful places to see on earth if you hadn't read about them first in books? Papa says learn first, then explore."

"Papa says. Well I say you're a brownnoser, Moshe."

Moshe bristled at the insult—"Am not!"

But he was. Every evening, while preparing to go to sleep, Moshe would think about the next day's lesson and try to come up with questions that would make his father proud. Although the Rabbi encouraged Moshe to ask questions, he preferred to challenge one of the older *yeshiva* students for the answers.

****

The conversation in the Rabbi's study is hushed yet intense. Still, the Rabbi's voice remains calm. How is it that the Great Man has so much room in his heart for kindness, even when facing fear? Memories of an unusually warm spring day flood Moshe's mind where once he witnessed just such an act of kindheartedness.

The year was 1933, and a thirteen-year-old Moshe was perched on top of the woodpile picking off the leaves. Music, voices, glasses clinking, and children laughing filtered through the breeze outside. The celebration happening inside the house was marking the day that Moshe-Yaakov had become a man.

A man? At thirteen? He had studied for a year, worked with the Rabbis to learn his Torah and Haftorah readings for his particular *Shabbat*, memorized the melodies so that he could chant his *parsha*, and prepared to lead the men and *yeshiva* students in a spirited discussion. So why did his body feel the same at this minute as it did the hour before he was called to the *bema* to read from the Torah for the first time? He kicked a rock with his shoe.

"So, the *bar mitzvah* boy is too grown up to attend a silly party?" The voice was startling, undeniably familiar, and yet strangely foreign, coming from outside in the yard. The *Great Man*, the Rabbi—his father—was standing on the porch on the *outside* of the door.

"No, Papa, of course not. I am praying," Moshe lied.

Rabbi Lozinsky stifled a laugh. "I can see that. Well then, say your 'Amens' and join me for a walk."

"Ani Adonai eloheichem, Amen," Moshe rushed and jumped off the

woodpile.

The Rabbi added, "Amen," as the two headed out of the yard and into the woods.

Late afternoon had always been Moshe's favorite time of day to be outdoors. The deep golden light of the sun shimmered atop the tree leaves, casting purple shadows across the dusty pathway. Moshe called this time of day the *whisper hour*. As the breeze grew softer, fluttering the leaves in the canopies, there was a still, peaceful feeling as all living things began the routine of settling in for the upcoming night.

Rabbi Lozinsky seemed deep in thought and for a while, the two wound their way down the wooded path in silence. When he spoke, his voice echoed off the tree trunks and gave Moshe a start.

"Every day I study the lessons faithfully, and still the Torah has something new to teach me."

"Yes, Papa."

"Well, I'm proud of you Moshe, you gave me fuel for thought today."

"Really, Papa?" Moshe said, surprised.

"So why are you not in the house with your friends and family celebrating?"

"I don't think it's right to celebrate, Papa. I'm not feeling like I'm a grownup."

The Rabbi studied his son. "Ah, I see. Well, the birth year of thirteen was decided centuries ago when people didn't live as long, and so to guarantee a future for the Jewish people, they needed to marry and have their children at younger ages. Today, we aren't in so much of a hurry. So don't despair and you needn't rush growing older. The feelings will come, and when they do, Moshe, you will wish you were still a child."

Moshe stared at his father. "Do you, Papa?"

The Rabbi sighed, but his attention was diverted to a commotion occurring above the bough of the trees. A large, aggressive squirrel was in a fierce battle with a sparrow for homesteading rights to the tree limb that was occupied by her nest. The sparrow darted at the squirrel, pecking at his head.

"See that, Moshe? That is the great *Passer montanus* quarreling with a common tree squirrel. Foolish squirrel, one should never get between a mother and her children."

15

"A *Passer* what?"

"*Montanus*—fancy name for Tree Sparrow."

"You know about birds, Papa?" Moshe asked, amazed.

The big man chuckled, "There's no law saying I can't have an inquisitive mind about things other than Torah, Moshe."

The sparrow swirled around squawking, and the squirrel answered with a forceful cacophony of clicks and screeches. Suddenly the squirrel swiped at the sparrow and the nest tumbled to the ground below. Frantic, the mama bird dove, her hatchlings lay helpless under the tree on the soft dirt. Rabbi Lozinsky knelt down, withdrew his hands into his coat sleeves, and carefully placed the baby birds back into their nest. The mama bird fluttered around the Rabbi's head but strangely, didn't attack him.

"Moshe, come here. Take this nest, we will put it back up where it belongs."

Moshe ran to his father.

"Hold it carefully," the Rabbi continued, "I will give you a boost."

The Rabbi knelt and clasped his fingers together making a sling. Moshe hesitated.

"It's okay," his father urged as his large hands cradled Moshe's foot.

The hands felt soft and squishy, not the hands of a workingman forging molten lead over the roasting heat of a fire. No, these were scholars' hands, made to gently trace fingers over letters, sentences, paragraphs, discussions, arguments, and laws; chapters of a people's past and present; warmth wrapped around a small foot.

"Okay. I'm going to lift you up," the Rabbi commanded.

Moshe's head barely missed the tree limb. It was an effort to remain balanced on one leg while trying to avoid the mama sparrow that pecked at his head and squawked in his ears. He rested his other foot on top of his father's shoulder.

"Easy there, Mama," the Rabbi reassured the panicked bird, "we'll have your babies back home in no time."

Moshe's hands trembled as he lifted the nest up to the limb. He held his breath and secured the nest into the crook of a branch.

"Okay, Papa, we're good."

The mama sparrow fluttered overhead as the Rabbi lowered Moshe to

16

the ground, his strong arms wrapped around Moshe's waist. For a brief moment their bodies were locked together as one.

Moshe closed his eyes. All his life he had yearned for a simple pat on the head or a hug from the majestic man. This was a moment he hoped would never fade.

The two stood side-by-side, watching as mama sparrow surveyed the condition of her hatchlings. Satisfied, she settled in and began singing a song of gratitude.

"*Baruch Hashem,*" said the Rabbi, dusting the dirt off his hands.

Moshe studied his father with wonder. Today, this larger than life man opened his heart to tiny birds, and Moshe got a smile, a hug, and a pat on the head.

"So that was a very insightful discussion you led in *shul* today, Moshe. I'm talking about your thesis on the Blessings and Curses. God put the Curses in place to encourage us to live a more righteous and devout life. The Curses show us that if we deviate from the laws, there will be consequences. In the Torah, God makes life simple; there is a right path or a wrong path. We walk down one or the other. And yet, you constructed a different interpretation. I'm curious, how did you arrive at your conclusion that blessings and curses are symbiotic? That both can exist at the same time as one action?"

How can this man be both a Rabbi and a father? And, he is waiting for an answer? From me?

Moshe swallowed hard. "Levi wrote a letter to me that mentioned an American saying, and I have been thinking it applies to my Torah portion."

"And what is this American brilliance?"

"The grass is always greener on the other side of the fence."

The Rabbi looked around thoughtfully.

"I believe it is a metaphor, Papa," Moshe continued. "People are not contented with the blessings they have, instead they yearn for more. Many are not even satisfied with the rewards they have earned."

"True, many break the tenth commandment," the Rabbi sighed, "but there is a scenario where yearning for more can be good. Take the artist who endeavors to create an awe-inspiring work, the athlete who yearns to break the fastest record, and the learned man who strives to be en-

17

lightened. Achievement is a blessing, even if the goal is unattainable.”

“Achievement yes, Papa, but sometimes a blessing can turn out to be a curse. See, it is not that simple. I believe it isn't a case of either—or. I don't believe these are separate principles. I believe that one resides within the other; one triggers the other. So we have to not be hasty with our choices. We need to weigh our decisions carefully.”

“Ah, thus another of your American idioms, ‘Be careful what you wish for.’”

“Papa!”

“Ah, my *boychick*, you think these eyes only read religious writings? These ears aren't deaf, you know. I am aware of some American idioms though I admit they don't always cross the language barriers. I mean who really needs greener grass?”

Moshe looks at his father and laughs.

“So, in your speech you mentioned our dear Mr. Korsky. May he rest in peace. Go on.”

“Yes, Papa. Mr. Korsky had a good business, many sons and daughters, respect in our community. He was considered the best milliner in all of Vilna. Those were his blessings, but it was never enough. He needed a bigger house, more horses, more silver for his wife's table, a new coat every winter for each member of his family. So, he started buying cheaper material and forcing his workers to sew faster. Soon he had a shoddier product but charged his customers a more expensive price.

“When his business saw hard times,” Moshe continued, “he stole and cheated people until he lost everything and brought shame to his family. His blessings drove him to his destruction. I believe that God also wanted us to understand that if we misuse our blessings, then we will suffer consequences.”

“Ah, Moshe,” the Rabbi smiled and placed his arm around his son's shoulders. “You said when we started our walk that you didn't feel any differently today. You studied the Torah, interpreted the meanings, and related the lessons to your own world. In my eyes, there is the proof you are seeking that you are becoming a man.”

****

What happened that day in the forest with the sparrow was but a fleeting moment. Perhaps it was God's way of showing him that his father is a mortal being, capable of compassion in spite of his holy stature. Moshe wonders if the heart has finite space for compassion, and then the overflow is left as scraps to fill the beggar man's cup. His father, the Great *Rebbe,* possesses infinite patience for all things—except his children.

A young scholar turns in Moshe's direction and nods. The rest of the group is too immersed in their conversation to notice Moshe and Elana in the doorway.

"It isn't very long from now that Germany and Russia will be signing a pact to invade Poland. They will split it up, and they won't stop there," says one of the village men.

"Yes," another adds, "Latvia, Rumania, Lithuania, even Finland. No one is immune."

"The Soviets are commandeering the factories, silencing the press, and arresting the Jewish leaders. Time has run out, *Rebbe,*" warns a *yeshiva* student. "We must leave within a few days."

A youthful village man leans over a map that covers the surface of the large oak desk. "We board the train at Kaunas and travel through Lithuania, to Moscow. There, we switch to the Trans-Siberian Railroad that will take us to the port of Vladivostok. The trip will take about ten days. At the port we board a ship for Japan."

"Japan," whispers the Rabbi, "we might as well go live on the moon."

An elderly gentleman places a packet of visas onto the desk. He opens to a page containing two official stamps. "The Dutch diplomat stamped two hundred passports for our families to go to Curacao."

Resigned, the Rabbi frowns and strokes his beard, "Curacao."

The gentleman nods. "Yes, but that is really not our final destination. Curacao is one of the few countries that will let us in. I persuaded our Russian contact to grant our exit visas to leave Russia, however, we are missing our transit visa stamps. Tomorrow we will go to the Japanese consulate in Kaunas and get the transit visas."

"The *yeshiva* is prepared to leave first thing in the morning," the student interjects, "you, *Rebbe,* and the families will meet us at the train station in Kaunas in two days."

19

"I'm worried," says the elderly gentleman, "how do we keep *kashrut* in a foreign land?"

The Rabbi sits quietly for a moment. "Do you think Moses worried about keeping kosher when he wandered the desert for forty years? Have we learned nothing from the Egyptians enslaving the Israelites?"

The men fall silent.

The Rabbi continues, "Rivka has lit the candles, yes?"

The student peeks his head out the door and nods to Moshe and Elana as they quickly scoot out the rear door. He studies the shadows of candlelight flickering across the gilded wallpaper in the foyer.

"Yes, *Rebbe,* they are lit."

"And the sun—has it set?"

The student returns to the doorway to see a stream of yellow gold light pouring through the leaded glass windowpane and across the wood floor.

"There are still a few minutes until we welcome the Sabbath."

"Well, then, I won't be offending God," the Rabbi says as he tears off the yellow Star of David patch sewn onto his coat sleeve and tosses it down onto his desk.

The men freeze.

"I see my actions have surprised you. Well know this, I am a willing and humble servant of *Adonai* only, but I will not serve a man who is trying to rob me of my name or obliterate our faith. We are no longer welcomed in the land of our birth. We will find shelter in another."

One by one the cloth squares of tattered yellow stars are ripped from coat sleeves and settle upon the surface of the heavy oak desk where some disappear, slipping between the stacks of leather-bound books.

Chapter Three

Outside the house, Elana draws her shawl tightly against her chest, partially to ward off the cold, but mainly because in his presence, Moshe makes her body tremble. He looks at her and smiles.

Since Elana became a young woman they can't speak as freely as they could when they were children. Theirs is a secret friendship since Orthodox law prohibits young men and young women from socializing without an adult present. Moshe misses the days when they would sneak away from the house and play together in the woods.

It's too bad that Elana couldn't have been on his kickball team. Sometimes they would get into a wrestling match, with Moshe landing in a headlock. He remembers teaching her how to ride a bicycle and how to fish. In turn, Elana taught him the names of plants and not to be afraid of bugs.

Even though it was forbidden for young girls to study Torah at the *yeshiva,* Elana was better at debating the weekly *parsha* than his friends at school. Moshe knows that had she been born a boy, she would have single-handedly squashed his team in stickball, become a revered Talmudic scholar, and been his best friend.

There are times when he is in her presence that he finds himself questioning the purpose of some of the sacred laws. Elana is living proof that the female brain is in many respects smarter and more focused than the male's. If his father could read his mind, he'd be banished from the family forever. Maybe his older brother Levi made the right decision moving to America.

Moshe moves to the woodpile and retrieves a small box. "I want to show you what Levi sent me from America. I've been hiding it from my little sisters."

"What is it?"

Moshe unwraps a small snow globe. He flips it upside down, and then right side up. White flakes rain down upon the Golden Gate Bridge and the harbor in the San Francisco Bay.

"Levi says he can see this bridge from his living room window."

"San Francisco," she reads from the sign inside the globe. "It looks like a wonderful place. Does it get as cold as here?"

"I guess, since it snows," he says shaking the globe.

"How do you feel about leaving our home, Moshe?" Elana asks, watching the snowflakes float around the little snow globe harbor.

"I am very worried about my work, Elana. There is much that I haven't finished. Thank goodness Torahs don't have feet, or I would have a lot of chasing to do when we return," he laughs and hands her some firewood.

"I'm worried, Moshe," she sighs, "Mama cries all the time. She is upset that Papa will only let her take one suitcase. And she doesn't want the Germans to steal *Bubbe's* silver."

"I doubt Hitler—or the Russians—will have use for your *Bubbe's* silver platters," Moshe laughs, affecting a German accent. "Please, *fraulein,* may I interest you in a juicy *schweinebraten?*"

Elana waves him away, *"Ech, tref."*

Moshe likes her quick wit and how easily she'll play along. He hands her another log and his finger brushes the top of her hand. An electrical current pulsates throughout their bodies—their hearts quicken. Elana lets her hand linger just a little too long. The blood races up her neck and into her face. Her eyes become glassy and her cheeks glow red.

"Are you feeling okay, Elana?"

"Of course not," she says, holding the snow globe to her cheeks. "My hair is hot!"

"Ha, that's a good one," Moshe laughs, curling his index finger around hers. Her soft, round fingers intrigue him. Warmth envelops his body as he studies her face—*Raise your eyes. See me. Please be mine.*

Her eyelids flutter and lift. The deep, brown pools tease, the fragrance of her soap entices, and the pout of her mouth seduces. His lips brush hers. He tastes the olive and wine that she sampled before the Sabbath prayers. He pulls back and laughs, "You cheated."

Elana covers her mouth and giggles. "I was starving! I couldn't wait for the sun to set."

There had been kisses before, in the days when she would wrestle him to the ground and plant wet smacks onto his forehead. That was when girls were disgusting; now they are a mystery. She squeezes his hand and smiles. At this moment by the woodpile they pledge their everlasting love, and he gifts her his heart.

Akiva pokes his head out the screen door. "Moshe, Elana, come, it's time for dinner."

Elana quickly pulls her hand away and heads towards the door.

✳✳✳✳✳✳✳✳✳✳✳✳✳✳✳✳✳✳

The Lozinskis' Sabbath table is dressed in the finest embroidered cloth. At one end, the Rabbi stands at the place of honor; his sons stand on both sides. Elana's brothers and several of the Rabbi's students join them. At the far end of the table Rivka, Miriam, and their daughters, stand next to their seats. Miriam notices that Elana's face appears flushed.

"Are you unwell, Daughter?" Miriam whispers.

"Very well, Mama," Elana blushes. "I was carrying firewood. I got hot."

23

"Tch," Miriam clucks with disdain. "You must let the boys do the outside work."

"Yes, Mama." She smiles and steals a glance at Moshe.

The family gathers to sing 'Shalom Aleichem' as the Rabbi circles the table, placing his hands upon each child's head for a blessing. Elana admires the table, set with Rivka's finest bone china plates, crystal goblets, and sterling silverware. The place settings have been in the family for decades, passed down from one bride to the next. One day she will have the honor of setting such a table for her own family's Shabbat dinner.

She thinks about the ritual for preparing for the Sabbath meal. On the Wednesday prior, she will shop, bake, and prepare the soups. On Thursday, she will marinate the beef, which she will slow cook on Friday morning. On Friday, she will visit Mr. Penkowski's shop to purchase a fresh salmon and the bakery to buy her fresh baked *challah* bread. During the week, her daughters will help with the baking of cakes and cookies. Then, twenty minutes before sundown on Friday evening, she will fulfill her commandment and proudly gather her children to light the *Shabbat* candles.

Shabbat dinners are a time to reflect and relax, a time to come together as a family and a community. It is a sacred time to exchange ideas and tell stories. Elana smiles, imagining that the most brilliant Rabbis from all over the world will come to dine at her *Shabbat* table.

The *Shabbat* evening should be a time of joy, but tonight a veil of bitterness hangs over the hearts of the families. All this decades-old beauty is soon to be abandoned, left behind unprotected. Elana shudders.

Rabbi Lozinski lifts the spigot on the ornate sterling silver urn, and the deep red wine pours into twelve small cups.

The cups are passed and raised as the Rabbi leads the *Kiddush:* "*Baruch ata Adonai, elohenu melech ha-olam, b're p'ri hagafen.*"

The guests utter, "Amen," and each takes a sip.

Following the *Kiddush,* each member at the table washes his or her hands before the meal. Rivka pours water from a glass jug, first over each guest's right hand and then their left, while Elana follows with a bowl to catch the flow. The Rabbi wets his hands.

"*Baruch ata Adonai, elohenu melech ha-olam asher kid'shanu b'mitz-*

vo-tav v'tzivanu al netilat yadayim."

The group immediately sits and Rabbi Lozinsky reaches for a silver platter. Carefully, he removes the ornately decorated silk cloth covering the *challah* bread. He vaguely remembers his grandmother separating the gold and blue threads she used to stitch her design into the silk. He pauses to marvel at the perfection of her handiwork. The littlest child giggles that his father is taking so long. The others quickly shush him. No talking is allowed until after the eating of the *challah.*

The Rabbi smiles; he knows well the impatience of a hungry child. Slicing into the golden bread he recites: *"Baruch ata adonai elohainu melech ha'olam hamotzi lehem min haaretz."*

"Amen," the group says in unison.

This is Moshe's favorite part of the meal. The sweet smells of breads baking fill the home each Thursday. The wafting scent teases his senses and tries his patience, for as soon as the aroma reaches his second-floor bedroom, he knows he has a twenty-four-hour long wait until the hot, buttery sweet bread melts on his tongue.

Platters of brisket and poached salmon rotate clockwise around the table. There are three salads and a dish of potato *kugal.* Moshe helps the little ones with the servings.

"In this week's *parsha,"* the Rabbi says, "we read about the *mitzvah* of *mezuzah.* What is the meaning of the word *mezuzah?"*

The children squirm in their chairs—their hands reach to the ceiling.

"Yes, yes children. Kiva, you tell me."

"It means doorpost."

"Yes, and what is a *mezuzah?"*

"I know, Papa," says Sadot, the Rabbi's youngest daughter. Plain and studious, Sadot is happiest when she is left alone with her books. Her misfortune is that she, like Elana, was born female. The sight of all the young men entering the *yeshiva* to study makes her burn with envy, and the thought of being stuck the rest of her life in a kitchen is nauseating.

"Yes, Sadot, you may answer."

"The *mezuzah* is a piece of parchment that has two passages from the Torah written on it. A *sofer*—"

"Like Moshe!" interrupts Kiva.

"Yes, like Moshe," sighs Sadot, annoyed, "has written the passages

25

which are *Shema Yisrael* and *Vehaya*."

"Very good. Ah, my little daughter, you would have made a fine *yeshiva* student. Now why is the letter *shin* on the outside of the *mezuzah* cover?"

Kiva cannot contain himself. His arm shoots upwards beyond the length of his jacket sleeve. The crumpled letter flies out of his waistband, shooting across the *Shabbat* table and landing onto Rivka's plate.

"Nu? What is this, Kiva?" Rivka asks, looking at the envelope.

"Ah. I forgot. Mr. Bernstein gave me this letter to deliver to our family, Mama. It's from Levi in America!"

Rivka looks at the envelope and sighs, "I will put this away until the Sabbath is over."

She stands and heads towards the heavy oak credenza.

Her husband motions to her. "Rivka, I know we are forbidden to partake in reading anything other than the study of Torah during the Sabbath," he says, "however, these are not the times that our forefathers imagined when they received these laws from God. Therefore, I am making an exception. We need some good news. Hand me the letter."

Rivka pauses just a moment to examine the brightly colored stamps and admire the neatly penned address.

"Baruch Hashem," says the Rabbi, staring at the envelope, "it has been too long since we've heard news from our firstborn."

Heightened anticipation fills the room as they watch the Rabbi carefully open the envelope along its seams. As he slides out the folded pages of the letter, several magazine ads float to the floor and a small photograph slips onto his plate. He leans forward. The chatter around the table falls silent as the muscles on the Rabbi's face tighten.

"Please, Papa," says Moshe, "the letter. What does Levi say?"

Rabbi Lozinski pushes up his glasses that have slipped down onto the bridge of his nose.

"Uri," says Rivka, "you want us all to expire from the anticipation?"

The Great Man sets the folded letter down on his plate; the photo floats onto his chair as he stands. No one moves, not a word is said. They watch him leave the dining room. The click of the study door echoes through the foyer.

Chairs fly. The group huddles. Moshe bends down, snatches up the papers off the floor, and discreetly places them into his pants pocket. Akiva swipes the photo off his father's chair. On it, a young couple poses with the Golden Gate Bridge in the background. The young man is dressed in a business suit and hat. One arm drapes around the bare shoulders of a young woman whose golden hair frames the delicate features of her face.

"It's Levi, Mama," Akiva says.

"Uh, what happened to his beard?" Rivka utters with surprise.

"Who's the lady, Mama?" Sadot asks. "She looks like an angel."

Rivka can feel the rise of her blood pressure—*This can't be possible!* Levi, her first born—her hope for their future in America—with his arm around a sleeveless flowered dress! *Bare arms. Outrageous!*

A black leather belt is cinched tightly around the young lady's slender waist—*What is she? An actress? A prostitute? Or worse—a shiksa?*

"Akiva, Sadot! Get your instruments and play something!" Rivka orders. "Everyone sit. Eat. The food will get cold!"

The children look confused. "During *Shabbat,* Mama?"

Rivka's mind is spinning. "Yes, yes. Just play."

"What do you want us to play?" Akiva asks, grabbing his violin.

Sadot returns with her viola and joins her brother.

"Anything—something soft and sweet but nothing mournful. Go ahead."

Strains of Bach drift around the room as Moshe watches his mother fuss with the serving platters. He stares at the photo of Levi standing beside the young lady. With one click of a camera shutter, Levi has managed to tip the family's world on end.

The mood at the Sabbath table is now awkward. Until the photo arrived from America, life in the *shetl* had been consistent and predictable. Propriety was well established. Rules followed without question. Looking at the photo in his hand, he cringes. Staring back at Moshe is his clean shaved brother and the bare-armed girl—the two, frozen in a moment of modernity.

27

Chapter Four

The light is harsh, grey, and hurts the eyes. Night has not quite ended, and morning is late to appear when the Rabbi and his family arrive at the Vilna train station. Low-lying fog hugs the steel tracks. Families unload their baggage while mothers wrap their sleepy children in their shawls to ward off the chill.

Rivka studies the trunks and cases. Her sigh is audible. The night before, she cleaned and straightened up her beloved house. Though her husband implored her to come to bed and get some rest, she was intent on leaving a tidy home. Never will anyone find a speck of dirt on the floor or dust on a cabinet shelf. Never, not even the Germans.

As of last night, that was the one part of her world still in her control. Rivka thinks about her clothes that she left neatly lining the upstairs bedroom closet, the children's toys inside the toy chest, and her husband Uri's books standing at attention on the library shelves. Every cherished family treasure tucked neatly into its place—waiting for the family's return.

"Moshe, I fear we will never see our home again," Rivka sighs.

"Mama," Moshe whispers, "we are all together, and that's what matters."

Rivka wipes her face and smiles at the sleepy girl in her arms.

"Are we going on our trip today, Mama?" the little girl asks.

"Yes, my sweet. We have an exciting journey ahead."

"Will I get ice cream?"

"Moshe, do you still have a piece of candy for your sister?"

Moshe reaches into his pants pocket and pulls out a striped peppermint. His sister's eyes widen as she grabs for the candy. All is forgotten when cool mint and sweet sugar mix on the tongue.

The families huddle on the platform with the group of students from the Rabbi's yeshiva. "When we get to Kaunas," says one of the older students, "we will go to the Consulate and get the proper stamps for our traveling visas. I hear the Vice-Consul, Mr. Chuine, is very sympathetic to our situation. There shouldn't be an issue."

In the dewy morning haze, Moshe sees Elana sitting on the platform deck. Her feet dangle over the side, swinging like an impatient little girl's.

"Your feet won't get the train to come any faster," Moshe says, as he sits down beside her.

"I hate this waiting, Moshe. It makes my skin crawl."

"Here," he offers. "Have a peppermint."

Reaching into his pocket for the candy, the magazine ads fall onto his lap.

"What's that?"

"Magazine advertisements. Levi sent them with his letter. He got a job in San Francisco to be a manager in a department store. It has a strange name—Gumps."

"Gumps!" she laughs.

"Gumps, Gumps, Gumps," they say in unison.

"How silly, Moshe, I want to go there and buy silly things. Okay, now show me the magazine advertisements."

In the photograph, a woman with bright red lipstick holds up a ketchup bottle and looks amazed.

"What is this?" Elana says, reading the copy aloud. "'*So easy a woman*

30

can open it.' That is ridiculous! Of course, a woman can open a ketchup bottle. Are American women weaklings? Tch. Show me the next one!"

Moshe unfolds the second piece of paper where two young women in bathing suits lounge beside a swimming pool. Moshe quickly scrunches the paper, but Elana grabs it before it can disappear back into his pocket.

"Look, this woman is smoking a cigarette. She is practically naked!"

"I'm sorry, Elana, this is not appropriate for you to see. I shouldn't have shown you these ads."

"Nonsense, Moshe. I've seen bare shoulders—my own," she laughs at Moshe's embarrassment. "And I am much smarter than those American women. I know how to wear clothes and I can certainly open a ketchup bottle!"

Her persistence is so amusing that he leans forward and accidently kisses the tip of her nose instead of her lips. Elana jerks back and laughs. "Ha, ha, you missed!"

"Uh oh, sorry, sorry. That was a mistake," he admits, turning red and looking around.

"Mistake? Uh-uh, I don't think so," she scolds, pulling his face closer and plastering his cheeks with little kisses. "Squirrel kisses," she laughs.

His heart is racing, and his giddiness is surprising. "Elana, stop. We aren't kids anymore. Someone will see us!"

"You don't like me anymore, Moshe? Since last night?"

"Shh ..." he smiles.

How he wishes he could tell her how he feels about her, but there are strict rules and protocols that must be followed. First, he has to get permission from his father, and then the families have to have a meeting. Considering the current situation, his declarations will have to wait.

Perhaps when they reach their new home in Kyoto, Moshe will find a beautiful spot overlooking an ocean and tell Elana how much he loves her. She will like that. He will seek out a diamond trader and purchase the brightest stone for her ring finger. He will take her hands in his and finally, after so many years, tell her how she lights up his world.

Akiva scuttles through the sea of anxious passengers waiting for the train to arrive. He joins Moshe and Elana at the edge of the platform.

"Moshe, is that smoke in the sky?"

31

"No, Kiva, it's just the fog."

Akiva pulls on Moshe's coat.

"Kiva, stop fidgeting," says Moshe. "Do you need me to take you to the restroom?"

"No, Moshe, I need you to look at that cloud. It's growing bigger and darker."

Moshe turns his attention towards the sky above the station. He starts, stabbed by a horrible sensation.

Elana senses his concern. "Moshe, what is it? What's wrong?"

"That's coming from the direction of the synagogue," he says stunned, "and that *is* smoke!"

The crowd stills, watching the cloud punch through the fog, emitting sparks of yellow-orange. Rabbi Lozinski raises his fist to the heavens and lets out a yell. Women grab their children and cry. The *yeshiva* students huddle close to their Rabbis.

"Moshe," cries Akiva. "The Baby! You have to save the Baby! Please, please!" he screams.

Moshe looks to his mother. Rivka pleads. "No, Moshe you must stay with us!"

"Mama, you and the family go to Kaunas and get our visas."

"No! This is the only train today," she implores.

"I will get on the first one out tomorrow morning."

"Wait, Moshe, I'll go with you!" Akiva says.

Moshe kneels down on one knee. "Kiva, you must stay and look after Mama and our sisters."

"Save the Baby, Moshe! Promise!" Kiva's breathing is rapid.

Elana rests her hand on Moshe's shoulder. "Promise," says Elana.

Moshe stands and tucks his ticket into his inside pocket. He locks eyes with the sweet face he has secretly loved for many years. "Yes," he whispers. "I promise."

Chapter Five

From his vantage point, high above the polished marble floors and the thick concrete columns, the double-headed golden eagle reigns fiercely over his domain. Sunbeams float through the stillness of the great room, reflecting off the gilded carvings of animals, plants, and religious icons that adorn the ark.

There is an unusual stillness—no songs of praise or prayers to God wafting up to his perch two stories high. No worshipers *dovaning*, swaying to their internal rhythms. The silence is palpable, and the two-headed eagle is on heightened alert. It was but a few minutes prior that the harsh slam of the heavily weighted front door awoke him from his slumber.

Multiple pairs of boot heels clack against the shiny marble as they scoot across the cavernous space. There is shouting of words strangely familiar, yet foreign. A foul odor emanates from the golden liquid splashing onto the pews, walls, and statues. One young soldier runs a trail of the liquid down the middle aisle, up the steps to the *bema* and the front of the ark. The soldier shudders beneath the eagle's icy glares. Then, he does the unthinkable. Throwing open the doors of the ark, he scowls at the scrolls and splashes the contents of the liquid onto the ornate Torah covers.

"I wipe you off this Earth," he shouts with a gush of vitriol. "I wipe you all away!"

He strikes a match. Satin and velvet explode. The eagle stretches one neck towards the soldier and screeches; the other head arches towards the heavens and cries. The deep blue velvet and embroidered satin material that shielded the scrolls for decades, disintegrates. Flames sear the parchment and the ink melts, dripping to the floor.

Moshe slips through a side door of the library and fights his way through a wall of smoke to reach the narrow staircase leading up to his studio. He knows all his work will soon become fuel to quell the hunger of the flames roaring below. Still, with the atrocity knocking at his door, the parchments, his inks, and his unfinished business push him to complete what he started—to save one little Torah.

Smoke obstructs his view and burns his eyes. Inside his studio he lingers; the air scorches his throat. He reaches for the small wooden box leaning against the corner of the far wall. He cradles the little Torah beneath his woolen coat. On the way out, Moshe grabs his silver *yad*, a bottle of ink, and his favorite quill pen.

With the fire licking at the sides of the staircase, Moshe takes a running leap and flies through the inferno to reach the floor below. In a heartbeat he is out the door, where fresh air fills his lungs. Broken glass crunches beneath his shoes. Windows of the Jewish owned businesses are smashed, the stores looted, while the non-Jewish owned businesses remain unscathed and display freshly painted signs in their windows—

"No Jews—No Dogs."

****

It is impossible to put a price on memories. Beyond Moshe's front door lives a treasure trove, silently waiting as he steps into the foyer of his family's home. So many of the household items have been formative in his life. Each one lovingly coddled by his mother and generations of mothers before. In the library, his father's beloved books fill the shelves, catalogued and archived for future generations to study. These great books contain the laws necessary to preserve a peaceful society and parables to inspire the pursuits of life's mysteries. But now, Moshe thinks, how would these great works explain this evil that has befallen his world?

At this moment he stands alone in the center of these precious treasures. Sadly, without his family, his community, and without Elana, his home has been transformed into a museum. These many items—meaningless.

Moshe heads to his bedroom and removes his heavy woolen coat. He is glad Levi isn't here to see it; the hem is singed and the coat reeks from the smell of smoke. Levi cherished the coat and was so proud when he purchased it with his savings from his work at Mr. Ruben's tailor shop.

The coat was Levi's parting gift to Moshe the night before sailing to America. Wearing it every day has kept close the brother he so dearly misses.

Oh, Levi, what words would you have for me now?—Moshe thinks as he gently settles the little Torah onto Akiva's bed.

"Akiva would want me to tuck you in and tell you a story," he says aloud to the Torah, "but it is you that has many to tell me, and I am at a loss for words."

****

Gone is the sunlight streaking across the hardwood floor. Silence haunts the hallways, the library, and the bedrooms with the void of a once active and happy family life.

Moshe wanders through the house alone, in the dark. Any light, even from a candle, could summon the devils that haunt the street outside.

Upstairs, he runs himself a bath and immerses his body into the warm water—*How ironic that for once I don't have to fight my brothers and sisters for bath time.*

Gentle and soothing, Moshe closes his eyes and lets the warm, soapy water pour over his body. He exhales one long, slow breath and feels his muscles relax, allowing him to drift into a peaceful sleep.

Elana laughs and pushes him onto the ground. At ten years of age, she is stronger than the boys at the yeshiva—*even stronger than Levi.*

He rises and chases her through the forest brush, but she disappears. Shielding his eyes from the glare of the sun, he sees her standing on top of a large boulder. The sun forms a halo illuminating her curly hair. She waves and calls to him.

Moshe runs to the boulder and slips his hands into a crevasse. One foot finds a ledge and he hoists his body upward. He is about to steady his other foot when the boulder begins to crumble.

Small pebbles slide from the top, raining down onto his face. A larger piece of rock tumbles down, scraping the skin on his hand. He starts to feel a vibration as he grabs tightly to the surface. He knows the boulder will soon give way under Elana's feet.

He yells to her to back away from the ledge, but she can't hear him and moves closer. The vibration gets stronger and the rumble—louder. The rock is crumbling. He must stop her. Moshe takes a deep breath, hoisting his body toward the top of the ledge—

His body flies out of the bathtub, spilling water onto the floor. Downstairs a china teacup crashes to the floor. He starts, awakened from his dream. The rumbling is real. Peering out the bathroom window, Moshe watches the tanks of the German army roll onto the street below. He grabs his undergarments and heads into his bedroom.

On the chair lays his woolen coat; on the bed sleeps the little Torah. Moshe knows he has to leave—*now!* Placing the Torah on the chair, he unrolls one end.

"Forgive me," he whispers, tearing off the wooden shafts that connect the bulky parchment and dropping them to the floor. Holding the frayed edge against his stomach, he rotates his body in a circle. The Torah begins to unravel. First come the Five Books of the Laws: *Bereshit, Sh'mot, Vayyikra, Bemidbar, D'varim.* Next come the *Prophets, Nevit'im, Joshua, Ezekiel, Kethuvim,* the *Psalms,* and *Proverbs,* which provide so much comfort during times of duress. Round and round flow Abraham, Isaac, Jacob, Ruth, Sarah, and wise Queen Esther; all the ancestors, laws, teachings, and stories wrapping around the waist of one Jew.

Moshe grabs the linen sash and secures the little Torah with a heavy knot. The sounds of commotion outside filter upstairs to his bedroom on the second floor. Moshe pulls the woolen coat over his body, runs down the stairs, and flies out the rear door. He passes the woodpile where his sweetheart brushed her hand against his and sealed their everlasting commitment. Heading into the forest, Moshe and the little Torah quietly slip into the darkness.

Part Two
Kaunas, Lithuania

Chapter Six

The people kept arriving, standing on the other side of the iron fence, hands clasped around the bars, looking in. He had heard all the pleas and the stories. He shared their tears; their fears left a sour taste in his mouth—*Those Jews. What did they ever do to anyone?*

Numerous times he had the pleasure of being the guest of honor at their Shabbat dinner tables. He had been moved by the gentle acts of kindness towards his family. Now these people were being diminished to the status of prey, hunted down and slaughtered.

Chiune Sugihara had written to his superiors in the Japanese Government. Three times he sent his plea to allow him to issue transit visas to Japan. Three times his queries were rejected. Instead, the order came to pack up his office, close up his house, and come home. He hopes he will be reassigned.

In the meantime, late in the evenings when his children are asleep, he wrestles with the two modalities that challenge his life—both involve issuing of the transit visas, an action which would be in direct violation of Japan's rules. Doing so would risk the penalty of imprisonment, and yet issuing the visas is the moral choice.

Rabbi Lozinski sends his two eldest students into the consulate with 200 visas to Curacao. Mr. Sugihara has seen this before. The visas could hardly be legitimate. He never believed Curacao would be the final destination for a large population of Polish-Jewish immigrants. Yet the stories of Soviet and German devastation—the fear of an annihilation of an entire race of people—causes sleepless nights. It was not Curacao that would be the end game; it was he, Chiune Sugihara.

On a normal morning when the sun is rising, the Kaunas train depot is bustling with travelers anxious to board their trains on time. Merchants load their wares of fresh fish and early baked breads while riders line up at the ticket windows purchasing round-trip tickets. A day will pass before the big steel monsters return passengers home to their families for supper.

Gathered on the platform, the Rabbi leads the men in a morning minion of prayer. In the marble appointed lobby, the mothers and eldest daughters do their best to keep the younger children occupied.

Elana knows this trip has been confusing for her younger sisters and brothers. It has been almost impossible to answer their never-ending questions—why can't I play with my dolls, why can't I sleep in my bed, why didn't Papa bring my books, will my teacher be angry that I'm missing school?

The answers are elusive. Elana wishes Moshe was here. He is so good at finding the right stories to soothe a distressed child. Right now, Elana's brain is as foggy as the air that surrounds her, and although it is September, she shudders.

The big hand on the wall clock snaps to the hour; it echoes throughout the lobby—*Where is he?*

She feels the vibration of the train rolling to a stop at the station. Passengers hustle, grabbing suitcases and children. The women join the men on the platform. A voice shouts through the loudspeaker.

Elana takes in a breath and listens to her mother's orders. "Elana, grab the hands of your sisters. Be quick. Go."

The older *yeshiva* boys help the Rabbi and his family board the train.

Akiva squeezes his body out the window.

"Wait, we can't leave! Moshe!" he screams. "Moshe hasn't come back!"

Elana looks up from the platform and sees the young boy dangling outside the train. She rushes to the window. "Kiva! Get back inside!"

"Moshe! Moshe!" Akiva struggles. "Tell them to wait, Elana! We can't leave!"

The train lurches forward. The boy slips, his body slides head first towards the tracks beneath the wheels. Elana grabs him around the waist; he dangles upside down.

"Hold on to me!"

One leg in and one out, the train lurches forward.

Inside the train car, two young men grab Akiva and pull him back into the car.

Akiva bangs on the window.

"Moshe!" he sobs. "No, please, no!"

Elana rushes to his side and holds him as he cries. She looks across the aisle to her mother—*How can mama be so calm? Of course, she has several babies to worry about; mothers never have time to be scared.*

She longs to be three years old, sitting on her mother's lap while traveling on a grand adventure. Instead, the evils that lurk outside this train taunt her. She resents that she has to be brave for the little ones and mourns the life she feels slipping away. Without Moshe there will be no wedding, no *Shabbat* dinners, and no children of her own.

"Elana, I'm afraid."

"Hush, Kiva," she whispers, "if you fear it, you'll make it come true."

The train wheels spin and pick up speed. The families settle in for the long ten-day journey. Elana draws a breath and watches her cherished home and her truest love fade rapidly into the mist.

Chapter Seven

The following morning the sky is clear and the wind teases the papers, visas, and passports that are so preciously guarded by the anxious families still waiting at the station. Mr. Sugihara sits at a folding table scribbling his name on the transit visas. He pushes through his exhaustion, shaking off the burn pulsating in his wrist. He has been writing for weeks, twelve hours a day, but he will not stop until the conductor announces the final boarding of the day.

Nervous travelers wave their passports in front of his face. The train will arrive soon, and he and his family must depart. Still, he will not stop stamping and signing until the big metal monster screams, jerks, and rolls away from the station.

Mr. Sugihara's wife, Yukiko, balances two suitcases while ushering their children onto the train. She turns to look at her husband—*I may have disobeyed my government, he told her, but if I hadn't, I'd be turning a blind eye to the very tenet for which I base my life; all life is sacred.*

Yukiko feels immense pride and at the same time, fear. If the Japanese and Russians find out that he is issuing visas—against their express orders—he and his family will be labeled traitors and will be executed. She turns towards the train, locking eyes with a young Jewish mother; both would give their lives for the safety of their children. She nods and steps to the side, allowing the young family to board.

Moshe steps off the train from Vilna and joins the anxious travelers at the Kaunas station. For once he is relieved to not find his family waiting in line—*They are on their way to Vladivostok. That is good. They are safe.*

A disembodied voice announces the arrival of the final train of the day that will take passengers to Moscow.

The crowd surges around the Vice-consul. Moshe clutches his transit visa—the official signature still missing. Mr. Sugihara rises from his table—hands claw at his suit coat—voices begging. Moshe's body is swept up and carried towards the train. The Vice-consul furiously signs the cards, dealing them out to the crowd.

It is startling to watch the only opportunity for freedom rest on the shoulders of the one man who has packed up his papers, secured his briefcase, and is about to disappear.

The platform shakes from the train engine's idling. Tempers flare and mothers cry. Static from the PA system competes with the shouts from the crowd. A scratchy voice announces the train's imminent departure.

Chiune Sugihara pushes his way onto the train and joins his family, who are settled in their seats. He furiously signs more visa documents. *Chiune Sugihara*—he curses the length of his name.

Frantic travelers pound on the windows from outside. The train's brakes release with a sudden blast of air and the cars jerk forward.

The crowd falls back.

Moshe is pushed face down onto the wooden platform. He stares at his non-valid transit visa. The steel wheels groan against the iron tracks, spewing an oily substance that burns his eyes. Someone steps on his hand.

"Get up!"

He hears his father's voice—or God's—or the stranger whose foot is cemented to the hem of his coat.

"Get up!"

The train begins to roll.

Chiune Sugihara slides down his window and thrusts his remaining signed transit visa cards into the air. Catching an updraft, they flutter high above the crowd.

The immigrants lunge, snatch, claw, and grab at the documents; their desperation roars mightily.

Moshe pulls himself to his knees, grabs onto the stranger's coat and pulls his body upright. His legs wobble.

The cards circle above, blocking the light.

Moshe shoots his arm straight up—high into the air—palm open. In an instant, the document folds into his hand. He clutches the signed visa card to his chest and looks at the sky. Tears burn his eyes. He squints towards the sun.

Tomorrow he will board an early train.

Part Three
Suzhou, China, 1939

Chapter Eight

"Aieeee," Master Zhao screeches, examining the piece of rice paper he slapped against the front windowpane inside his writing studio.

The sunlight pouring through the paper exposes every imperfection of each handwritten character and reveals the incompetency of the artist. A written character must contain balance within its structure—a strong skeleton, all sides symmetrical, the bottom half supporting the top, executed with kinesthetic brushstrokes, each character well-choreographed.

This has been the basis for every written document covering thousands of years; the technique requires a young student to dedicate his life to perfecting his artistry.

Near the feet of Master Zhao, a young boy crouches like a beetle; face down, back rounded on the floor. Master Zhao squints at the writing. Chinese characters stack in uneven vertical rows and the penmanship is sloppy.

"Garbage! Even my pigs are too good to live on this!"

Master Zhao crunches up the paper and throws it at the crouched boy. "Do you not care about my teachings?"

He looks over at his students who sit hunched over their writing tables.

"Sit up straight," Master Zhao commands. "Let the ink almost run out before it touches the paper. Watch your hand pressure."

Master Zhao goes to his writing table and retrieves a second piece of calligraphy.

"Look, son, this one," he says, pointing to a handwritten character on the paper. "What do you see?"

The young man raises his head, his eyes as dark as the two Chinese characters on the page.

"Do you not see the strength in the brushstrokes? Jian, do you not share the pride I felt as I painted this character on this paper?" the Master asks. "There is no pride in your work. It's lazy and gutless."

Lady Zhao, the Master's wife, scowls as she enters the room. "You," she points at her husband and then at the floor, "let up on the boy!"

"Ech," he counters, "how will he ever take my place when I'm gone?"

He turns his attention back to the crouching figure.

"Are you gutless? Where is your pride? Look up, look up now! What do you see?" he asks, holding out the paper to his son.

The teenager raises his head, drilling his eyes with an intensity that forces his father to step backwards. "I see lines on paper, Baba, but unlike you, I do not see the tiger hiding beneath."

Then, without obtaining his father's permission, Jian rises and runs out of the studio.

Master Zhao looks to his wife and breathes a heavy sigh. His face falls.

"You push our son too hard," Lady Zhao sighs. "Jian, is a sensitive boy."

"You coddle him too much," he whispers. "Laziness will not be tolerated in the house of Zhao!"

Ming-Hua, Jian's younger sister, shivers and wraps her arms around her body. She knows Jian is running again. A rush of energy causes a breeze to brush her face as he flies past.

It wasn't worth calling out his name. He would never stop. Instead, he will jump down the graded embankment and follow the riverbank until the path meets the forest. There, he will head into the dense woods and disappear.

****

In the year of the Rooster, 1921, Zhao Shu and her husband, Zhao Heng were about to become first-time parents. Lady Zhao's position in society—as the wife of an esteemed poet and historian—afforded her the luxury of having the birth at home, surrounded by a midwife, nurses, maids, and family. Lady Zhao's bedroom was beautifully appointed with floral silk-lined walls, Persian carpets, and delicate china vases—heirlooms from both families.

Zhao Shu was very proud that she would be bringing honor to the family by giving birth in a fashionable setting. What she didn't anticipate were the long hours of labor.

In the beginning, at the first twinge of a contraction, the midwife guided her outside for a long walk along the banks of the canals that weaved throughout the older section of the city.

As a young bride, Zhao Shu delighted in exploring her new home that possessed magnificent ancient gardens and the reputation for being the "Venice of the East." However, at this moment the anxiety of her child's impending birth made her yearn for Beijing, her childhood home. Beijing was an active city with the best doctors available, and there she would have the comfort of her parents and sisters.

Marrying Zhao Heng had meant moving to his familial home in Suzhou, a small village located in the Jiangsu Province along the shores of the Yangtze River, nine hundred miles away.

It had been a challenging adjustment, although her husband worked hard to ensure her happiness. She was presented with beautiful material for robes and dresses, and seamstresses to fashion them. He hired a cook to prepare her meals and maids to clean the house, and offered her a stipend to spend on whatever she desired. Her family was always welcomed and came regularly for visits in spite of the distance.

Zhao Heng was a kind and patient man to all who knew him, and yet he fiercely guarded his position as China's Master Calligrapher and

Poet. When mentoring young students, he could be a bull: tough, demanding, gruff, intimidating.

Like his grandfathers and father before him, he carried a heavy weight. Previous relations represented the voice of their generations and of the Emperors. They were the archivists entrusted to ensure that the legacies of the dynasties endured forever.

During years of upheaval, battles, and strife, Zhao Heng's ancestors put brush to paper and captured the spirit of the times. Calligraphy represents the highest form of Chinese art. The artist doesn't pick up a brush, dip it in ink, and press it to paper unless he knows what content will flow. Each stroke has purpose and must be deliberate. The permanence is a huge responsibility, and for that, Master Zhao has earned the right to be a bull.

Lady Zhao was never on the receiving end of her husband's impatience and therefore was content to play the role of dutiful wife, to bear and raise his children. Their relationship was rooted in traditional Chinese customs and its origin, a proper courtship. Their first kiss was on their wedding night.

When they were first introduced, she felt nervous because of his demeanor. Handsome in face, he stood taller than her father and was several years older than she. He would take the train 900 miles to visit, and with her chaperones nearby, he would speak quietly about his life.

When he returned to Suzhou, as his affection for her grew, he would write her letters filled with poems describing his village. His words brought to life the images of fishermen, willow trees lining the banks of the Yangtze River, and ancient canals flowing under stone bridges. She yearned to walk through the meticulous gardens surrounding his family's ancestral home and see the stars blanketing the night sky.

She savored every letter and committed to memory each line of poetry he wrote. At night, she would sit by her window and whisper his lines with the hope that he would hear her voice in the wind.

Zhao Shu was convinced that Heng knew her better than her own sisters. His words captured her joys, her sadness, her strengths and weaknesses. His admiration touched her deeply.

Each night before lying in her bed, she would unfold a small piece of rice paper and trace the characters of a poem he had written in her honor. Perhaps over the distance he would feel her gentle fingers brushing against his face.

> *Your heart spun of sugar,*
> *forbearing in the sun,*
> *vanishing in the rain.*

She etched his words upon her heart.

In her family, being the middle of five siblings she held no position of prominence. Her parents were busy doting on her two older brothers, so Shu felt invisible. This courtship changed everything. Now someone saw her as lovely and cared about how she felt. Even her parents began to take notice of their daughter.

After a while, she began to look forward to his visits. She appreciated being in the presence of a gentleman who shared his worldly knowledge. The girls were never allowed to participate in political or philosophical discussions, but in Heng's company, she was encouraged to speak out loud the thoughts which were built up in her mind. Best of all, he listened.

One afternoon, in a park near her home, Heng pointed to a flock of geese.

"What do you see in that pond?"

"Well, I see a flock of geese," she answered.

"Yes, watch how they move. See how they arch their necks with a gentle sway?"

His hand fluttered though the air mimicking the movements of the geese as they swam.

She was fascinated by the rhythm of the designs his hands created in the air. Making certain that the chaperones were preoccupied, he gently took her hand and guided it through the air, mirroring the movements of the graceful birds.

"There, you just wrote *xiong*." Looking over and pointing at the elderly, grumpy chaperone, he whispered, "bear."

Shu giggled, and she was hooked—fascinated. Never had she met a person who possessed the ability to see the world the way he did. She felt honored that he chose to spend these days with her. That night, she told her sisters that one day she would become Lady Zhao.

Zhao Shu found the honor of carrying the Great Poet's offspring daunting. Her belly was so swollen she couldn't see her feet, and walking was difficult without the aid of the old midwife.

"Perhaps we should turn back? I fear we have gone too far from the house," she worried.

"Nonsense. Walk, and the baby will come," scolded the midwife.

The women paused at the top of a stone bridge and watched the *sampans* glide silently underneath. The lapping sound of the water lulled her into a temporary moment of peacefulness, remembering the past and her husband's first description of the fishermen sculling their long poles that guide their boats down the canals and rivers.

The beginning of 1921 had brought major changes to her serene life. She was keenly aware of the stress her husband and the families were feeling of late. Her parents in Beijing wrote many letters describing the famine that afflicted their provinces. The military forces in the north and south of China were constantly at odds and engaged in a struggle for control of power.

Zhao Heng worried that his work as a Master calligrapher would no longer have purpose. It tore at his soul to think that after countless centuries of his ancestors' dedication to the art, the reign would end with him. His beloved country was mired in political turmoil.

The ugly infighting between the warlords in the north and the warlords governing the south were choking his tranquil life. He had also been reading that a group of young men living in the French Concession in Shanghai were forming a party true to the beliefs of communism. Should this party come to rule it would belie his Buddhist beliefs and practices.

Zhao Shu was fearful for her husband and her family. At times the uncertainty would bring on cramps, and the midwife and nurses would flutter around her, barking orders and forcing long rests in her darkened bedroom.

Zhao Heng decided that no one was allowed to speak to his wife about politics or hardships while inside the house. It was vital that his wife would have a good birth and produce a healthy heir. Although at times, he would watch the river flow and wonder—*What kind of world am I bringing new life into?*

The old midwife pulled a white Lotus flower from her bag. "Here," she said, handing Lady Zhao the flower, "float this Lotus in the river. You will have a strong, healthy son!"

"A big one at that," Lady Zhao laughed, tossing the flower off the bridge. It landed on the water, upside down.

"Tch," clucked the midwife.

Lady Zhao gasped and rubbed her belly. She planted her feet firmly onto the slate-clad walkway, being careful not to turn her ankles or ruin her velvet slippers.

The old midwife was right, the walking was a good deterrent from the pain, however, the contractions were coming faster, and they must get home.

In the year of the Rooster, babies are punctual.

Chapter Nine

The boy came out kicking, cocooned in a mass of sticky goo. He announced his arrival with a hearty scream. The girl slipped out into the arms of the old midwife almost unnoticed. Two babies!

Unexpected, but not totally a surprise since Lady Zhao had confided to the midwife that she thought she had felt more than one set of feet kicking at her insides.

What a blessing! Honor to the house of Zhao!—she thought, swelling with pride. She looked around the room expecting celebratory coos and smiles. The air stilled. The nurses froze where they stood. An aura of silence shrouded the room.

"This baby—a girl—is damaged," the midwife spat.

The small crowd of nurses, maids, and family members huddled around the bedside. A nurse helped Lady Zhao sit to an upright position.

"Bring her to me, let me see," Lady Zhao demanded.

Delicate and petite, the baby girl slept quietly, unaware that her right foot was no larger than a seamstress's thimble. Lady Zhao cried out.

Maids rushed to draw closed the thick velvet curtains covering the large windows. The bedroom door was bolted shut.

"Eh, born with a Golden Lotus," the midwife scoffed.

Lady Zhao's mind spun. How dare this old midwife utter words that were associated with perversion and erotica—*Inappropriate and despicable!*

"Get out of my room now!" Lady Zhao screamed.

"But Madam," the midwife protested, "you must not get attached." She turned to a nursemaid. "Take this one to the nursery!"

"No!" Zhao Shu yelled. "Did you not understand me? I told you to leave! Leave my house this instant!"

The old woman collected her things, bowed low, and walked backwards out the door. Zhao Heng was waiting in the hallway, aware of the commotion.

"You have one healthy son, though two babies were born," the old midwife hissed. "Leave the damaged one by the riverbank or throw her into the Yangtze. Do not keep a girl with a lily foot. Keeping such a child will bring you misery and shame."

When Zhao Heng stepped out the front door to address the crowd of excited neighbors waiting in the yard, he held only the boy in his arms. Zhao Shu stayed in her bed and wept. How could karma be so cruel?— *Have I not been the perfect daughter to my parents? Didn't I honor my family by marrying China's most respected poet, one whose legacy dated back to the Song dynasty?*

This birth should have been a grand occasion. Immediately, close family and the nurses began encouraging the parents to give up the girl.

"A damaged child brings hardship and bad luck to a family," a nurse warned.

"Listen to me, daughter, this girl baby will be your burden the rest of your lives," cried Lady Zhao's mother.

Zhao Shu looked at the bundle wrapped up in her arms. The midwife's words were true. Those unfortunate ones born with physical deformities were forced to live their lives on the streets as beggars.

For girls, life would be spent in servitude—or worse—in the sex trade. A female born with a small foot would be the treasured prize for men with certain sexual perversions. In the Chinese culture a damaged child

60

was considered an obstacle to ensuring the genetic "quality" of the population.

The thought that Zhao Shu created a malformed baby made her sick and frightened. No young man from any of the prestigious Chinese families would be allowed to marry her daughter. If she were lucky, perhaps her daughter would become a maid or a nanny. Zhao Shu thanked Buddha that this affliction spared her little son who would grow up ensuring his filial duty, supporting them as they age.

A nurse gently lifted the little infant from her mother's arms and left the room. Zhao Heng returned with his newborn son and joined his wife on the bed. They gazed at the sleeping child—so many hopes, dreams, and plans rode on this tiny life. But, the girl?

Zhao Shu looked up at her husband—his expression strong and resigned.

"Bring the girl," he ordered the nurse.

"Oh, husband. What did our little daughter do in her life before that would bring such a punishment?"

"Hush, this is not a matter of punishment. Karma does not decide the development of a baby in the womb. This child can still grow to be a healthy person."

The nurse returned with the infant girl and placed her into Master Zhao's arms. He stroked her forehead, and she wrinkled her nose and yawned. He unwrapped the cloth blanket swaddling the baby and cradled the tiny foot.

Though many people in his country believed that a child born disabled was damaged and therefore not worthy of a normal life, Zhao Heng possessed a profound respect for all living beings. Perhaps his position as China's esteemed poet had given him the confidence to remain steadfast in his morality. And now, with the birth of this special child, he had been issued a challenge.

Whatever the reason, he was resolved—and would demand acceptance from his family and his community—to respect both his children equally. His burden would be to dedicate energy with his work to secure a larger dowry so that perhaps, when she came of age, he would be able to buy her a husband.

"Shu-Shu, we must bless both these children with a lifetime of good fortune. This little one will pick up any negative feelings, and that will place a larger burden on us all. Do we all understand what I'm saying?"

He set his gaze on each nurse, maid, family member, and finally his wife. "And, open the curtains. Our children will not be raised in a cave!"

A nurse wiped the tears off Lady Zhao's cheeks. Zhao Heng brought his infant daughter to the window. He caressed the sweetness in her face.

"Today you look many years younger, husband," Lady Zhao whispered.

"I am, my sweet Shu-shu," he smiled. "I have been blessed twice over."

Master and Lady Zhao would raise this child, educate her, and hope for the best. Heng named his son Jian and his infant daughter Ming-Hua —*tomorrow's flower*.

Chapter Ten

Ming-Hua lived for the sounds of the children's laughter. It meant they were having fun kicking balls and chasing each other through the immaculate gardens surrounding her home. For the first few years of her life, little Ming would sit on her nursemaid's lap and watch the children play.

Born only five pounds, she was easily carried from room to room or strapped to a nanny's back when they went outside for a walk. Ming loved the outdoors and would become inconsolable whenever her daily walks were canceled due to a rainstorm.

Inside the ancient home, Ming and her twin brother Jian lived like royalty. Nurses, maids, and cooks tended to their needs, and tutors marveled at how quick and accomplished the twins were with their lessons.

Ming especially loved geography, memorizing the capitals of each country and the names of each ocean. She was fascinated with people who lived in lands with topography so different from China. She favored books describing different cultures; foreign lands where people wore strange clothing and ate unusual cuisines. She laughed when she learned that the Americans were in love with their automobiles.

Most of the homes in her village bordered the shore of the Yangtze

River or the narrow streets adjacent to the canals. Ming's house was built on a large property; a land grant gifted to her ancestors from Emperor Taizu, centuries ago. It was located five miles outside of the center and hosted one of the premiere gardens in the province.

The children of the village enjoyed their days getting lost amongst the trees, flowers, waterfalls, and ponds. Lazy days were spent playing with fortune sticks under the small pagoda in the center of the garden.

Though prohibited by their parents, Jian and his friends delighted in slipping away from their nannies and exploring the forest at the edge of the property. Theirs was a world filled with joy and harmony, sheltered from the horrors that haunted the adults and threatened their futures.

****

As the twins grew, Lady Zhao made it her mission to prepare her son for his eventual responsibility as China's Master Calligrapher. She spent most of her days teaching her children how to write the Chinese characters. Ming loved the feel of the brush in her tiny hand.

For Jian, the long hours of memorizing thousands of characters made him restless and the smell of the ink—nauseous. Instead, his passion lay with the artisans who could turn a block of wood or a boulder of stone into an intricate carving. Sometimes he would slip away from the house and watch the master wood carver, Master Guo, at work. Eventually, he gained the trust of the artist and was invited to apprentice and learn.

Ming knew of Jian's secret but promised never to discuss the subject with Mama or Baba.

One morning, Ming awoke to find Jian carving into the sash framing her bedroom window. Birds, butterflies, vines dripping with lilies, and a rooster, their birth sign, sprang to life. Each animal and flower exquisitely detailed.

"Jian, how beautiful! Were you here all night?" Ming asked, wiping the sleep from the corner of her eyes.

"Most of it," he answered, yawning.

"What a wonderful surprise. Help me to the window."

"I see you every day sitting inside your room wishing you could join the fun," he said, "so I brought the garden in."

Jian helped Ming hop over to the window where she sat down and traced her finger along the outlines of the carvings embedded into the windowsill.

"I can hear the breeze blowing in the vines and the song this bird is singing," she mused.

"Now you won't be lonely, Ming. This bird sings only for you."

Ming threw her arms around her brother. It had been a long time since she felt happiness.

****

At the age of nine, Ming had grown too heavy for the nannies to carry. Her greatest wish was to be able to run, to jump into the pond, to pick up her feet and not fall down, to travel in a forward direction and take herself to the shops without the aid of her nanny.

Ming despised her tiny foot, cursing at it when the nanny wasn't nearby. In her mind she saw it not as a small deformity, but rather a heavy anchor weighing her down, a life sentence to be served wasting lonely days in her silk-walled prison.

In the afternoons, when the children's laughter seeped through her window, Ming had her easel and paints for company. She found the views of the garden a compelling subject. If she couldn't join Jian and his friends, then she would paint them. In time she had a nanny set her up under the pagoda by the koi pond or outside in front of her home.

Eventually, Ming had her parents' permission to go into town with her art supplies. The excitement of new scenery overrode the embarrassment of being pushed in a cart down the cobblestoned pathways. The people passing by would wave and then whisper.

In the village, her watercolors captured the scenes of the boats drifting down the river, of the willow trees and the mountains in the distance. She painted Mr. Li in front of his bookshop, the vegetable vendor with his cart, and the beggar asleep in the doorway of the grocery.

Preferring to use raw silk for her canvases, Ming experimented with the material and how it absorbed the color and inks. Her canvases captured light filling the skies with rich sunsets or ominous rain clouds. She found her voice with each stroke of the brush. Shops, houses, and bridges consisted of bold, thick lines contrasting the delicate strokes that fashioned birds, flowers, and villagers. She learned that applying pressure on the brush allowed her to control the texture. Emulating the rich color pallet of her village, images flowed from her hand onto the silk. Her paintings were subtle, fluid, and lyrical.

Soon the family began to notice her work. Zhao Heng pronounced, "Ming was born to the wrong sex. She would have made a great Master Calligrapher."

Ming took his statement as a compliment, for any attention from her father made her more determined to achieve perfection with her art.

****

Having a physical disability meant that Ming's bedroom could not be located upstairs where the rest of the family slept at night. There were times, when the house was quiet, that the night sounds kept her awake. She would worry—if the beggars came into her house while the family was asleep upstairs, how would she be able to run to safety? It was on those nights, when her worst fears caused her to grip tightly to her quilts, that Jian would magically appear in her room.

"What is wrong, sister?" he would ask her.

"What if they come?" Ming shuddered.

"Who?"

"The beggars—what if they come to take me? How will I run to Mama and Baba?"

Jian joined his sister on her bed. He smiled and gently patted her leg.

"Don't worry, Ming. I will make sure no one hurts you—no one, ever."

"How will you know? You sleep upstairs. No one can hear me down here."

"I heard you," he smiled, pointing to his head. "I'm here now, right?

66

You don't need to worry. Now go to sleep. Teacher will be quizzing us tomorrow on our English and geography. Are you ready?"

"Yes, Jian. I've memorized twelve new words and seven new capitals."

"Good, I am leaving Earth's nightlight on for you."

He opened the drapes to let the moonlight streak across the walls of her bedroom. Then, as silently as he appeared, he slipped out of her room. Ming smiled at the moon shining brightly through her leaded glass window and wondered—*What would the name of your capital be?*

✶ ✶ ✶ ✶ ✶ ✶ ✶ ✶ ✶ ✶ ✶ ✶ ✶ ✶ ✶ ✶

The day of their tenth birthday should have been a big celebration for the twins. For years, their aunties from Beijing would tell stories about birthday parties held in large halls or grand hotels.

The parents of the children would provide a feast consisting of many courses. Guests numbering in the hundreds would applaud as waiters, dressed in crisp black jackets, paraded into the hall carrying silver platters high above their heads.

The birthday child's name would be announced, and she or he would make an entrance—the boy dressed in an embroidered robe or the girl in a long silk dress. Musicians would play traditional Chinese music.

One auntie bragged that her parents were so wealthy they hired drummers, a fire dancer, and a large papier-mâché dragon to dance and entertain the guests. Traditionally, the child received money wrapped in red paper, or special gifts of embroidered silk, gold, or silver, but this was 1931, and the Japanese had invaded Manchuria. The family was concerned that the opulence of an elaborate celebration would be disrespectful to those suffering in their homeland; a party was out of the question.

As Zhao Shu gathered her children together on the morning of their tenth birthday, they could tell she had been crying.

"This is a very important day," she started, "and you know from my heart that I would want to mark this occasion with a big celebration."

67

The twins watched her in silence.

"I am sorry, my children, but that is not to be this year," she said with sadness in her voice.

Ming felt her face drop. She so desperately wanted a special day where she would be the center of attention. She longed to see admiration on the faces of her family and the invited guests.

"No party?" Jian asked.

"No, my son," Zhao Shu wept.

"Oh Mama," Ming sighed, "it is okay, really. What would I do with a party anyway? I can't dance."

Zhao Shu smiled gently. "You have a thoughtful heart, Ming-Hua. We will have a dinner, and in your honor, your grandparents and aunties will be arriving soon from Beijing."

"Will they bring presents?" Jian asked.

"Of course, Jian. Grandpa has a special surprise for you."

It was hard for Ming to feign happiness for the favorite son, even though Jian deserved all the accolades that he received. He was smart, athletic, talented, and kind to his sister. The other children in the village admired him, and no one dared to make a disparaging remark about Ming's disability for fear of being chastised by Jian. However, Ming couldn't help feeling jealous.

Zhao Heng insisted his family and household staff conduct their lives normally, as though there was no threat of an impending invasion. The rising Chinese Communist Party had recently become his main customer, and creating poetry exalting the greatness of their cause.

There were nights after dinner when he would quietly leave the house and follow the riverbank for five miles to the old Pingjiang Road. There in his studio, he found solace writing the characters that gave voice to the pain, suffering, and concern for his beloved countrymen.

Old China existed within the banners hanging on the walls, encircling him with the love of his ancestors and the serenity of his life in the past. Examining his work, he felt satisfied that the strength of the brush strokes forming the characters elucidated the rage he felt deep inside. He hated the invaders poisoning his country.

He questioned how man's thirst for power superseded human decency. Many of his poems questioned why—when man is given the gift of a peaceful and healthful life—is he not content? This issue was perplexing and kept him up most nights—*More power, more cruelty… never enough.*

Lady Zhao's family arrived from Beijing and settled into their rooms. In the afternoon there were tea and card games. Jian and Ming never let their eyes stray from their grandfather, who commanded the room from the faded French chair that had been a wedding gift from the Zhaos. The twins wondered if each word grandfather spoke might be a clue to Jian's fabulous surprise birthday gift.

The dinner that evening was modest but delicious. Cook presented several platters filled with freshly caught fish and meats. Ming and Jian were each given the customary bowls of long noodles, which when eaten, ensured a long and healthy life. Cook also baked a cake, artfully decorated with Lotus flowers.

After the meal was finished, the aunties presented the twins with eggs dyed deep scarlet, representing renewal. Grandma gave both children red envelopes containing coins. Zhao Heng carried out a large cardboard box and set it on the floor in front of Jian.

"Your grandfather brought you something special."

Jian pulled off the top of the box and reached inside. He began removing the contents: slightly rusted handlebars, two wheels, the tires—flat, a worn leather seat, and two well-worn pedals. Jian gasped at the rusty parts lying on the floor.

"This bike was mine when I was your age," Grandfather said with pride. "I rode it all over my village and now you will too. Tomorrow I will help you build your bike and teach you how to ride it."

"Thank you, Grandfather!"

Jian couldn't believe his luck. The bicycle would give him a means to escape the drudgery of his schooling and home life.

Ming studied the bicycle parts. They will be assembled into a wonderful gift that she can never share.

Chapter Eleven

"Your face is as red as a pomegranate," Ming laughed after watching Jian fall off the bicycle for the fourth time.

"It's the cracks in the pavers. They are mean to the tires," he snarled.

"Yes, of course." Ming knew her brother's limit before he would blow up, so she didn't push.

Jian threw the bike down onto the road. "I can't get the balancing right!"

"I wish I could try it," she sighed.

He was taking a moment to let his frustration pass when a thought occurred.

"Ming, stand up. I'm going to put you onto the seat."

"What? No Jian, I couldn't!"

"You are going to be my counterweight. Come here," he insisted.

Ming looked at the bike and then to her crutches. Weeks before, the bicycle had been Jian's special gift, but hers—a wheelchair. Baba had been so happy that he had found the wooden chair with the wheels made

71

of rubber. Mama had a local woman knit a pair of gloves so that Ming's hands would stay clean, and the local seamstress fashioned a cushion out of velvet. When Baba brought out the chair for the family to admire, Ming's eyes flooded with tears—that was the worst day of her life.

Ming hopped over to the bike. Her body shook as Jian slipped the crutch out from under her arm.

"Now, swing your foot over this bar. I will hold you."

"Okay," she said, pulling her leg over the top bar.

"Hop onto the seat. It's all right—I've got you. Keep your feet clear of the pedals."

Jian straddled the bicycle as Ming clung to his waist. He stepped down onto one pedal and the bike lurched forward. Three wheel rotations and the pair crashed into the wall of Mr. Lin's bookshop.

"Eh!" he yelled. "Hold on!"

"Please Jian, get me off!"

"Not yet, no! I can get this. I'm going to walk us down to the river-bank."

Ming clung to her brother—stuck between abject terror and the thrill of this new adventure. Jian steered the bike toward the riverbank. Ming braced herself as the wheels caught every fissure in the cobblestones. "Ah-ah-ah, Ji-Jian. Hur-hurry-e-e-e up-p-p," she giggled.

The road that paralleled the riverbank was smooth and flat. Ming waved to the fisherman on the shore who found the sight of the twins on an old bicycle amusing.

"Okay, we'll try this again. It should be easier now," Jian said as he swung his leg over the top bar and straddled the bike. "You okay?"

His face was flushed, and she knew that look. If they had to be there all night, he would never give—

"Ahhhh," she gasped.

The bicycle veered to the right and wobbled underneath them. Jian oversteered sharply to the left. He pulled his body upright and slammed his foot down hard on the upper pedal.

"Hang on!" he yelled back. The bike lurched forward with a smooth glide, racing the *sampans* floating on the river.

"We did it! Ming! Ming! We're riding!" he shouted.

Ming gasped, watching as the stores of the village flew by. The willow leaves became swirling masses of greens and yellows.

Adrenaline surged through her body. Her head pounded, and her heart quickened. She felt dizzy passing a flock of geese soaring along the riverbank. She closed her eyes, sensing her body in motion.

The speed, the thrill, and the novelty of gliding forward were exhilarating. Ming relaxed her grip on her brother's waist, holding out her arms.

Her fingers fluttered through the air.

For the first time in Ming's life she was moving forward without the aid of crutches, wheelchairs, or a nanny's arms. Each wheel rotation accelerated their speed, and in an instant, they had left the village and reached the edge of the woods. Motion had widened the borders that imprisoned her world. She threw back her head and laughed.

She had captured the feeling of freedom and made herself a promise to never let go.

Chapter Twelve

By 1937, The Warlords War between the north and the south had failed. The Japanese were marching through villages—pillaging, raping, and burning everything in sight. Their cruelty was unspeakable. Babies were torn from mothers' arms and thrown into the rivers. The mothers were burned alive.

The men who made up the various factions of the Chinese army were retreating and holing up in the mountains. The Warlords agreed they now had a fiercer enemy in the Orientals. The Japanese produced robotic soldiers who lacked a conscience and were capable of committing atrocities.

In Zhao Heng's world, such atrocities must not exist. He produced many poems from 1924-37, exploring the theme of acting without accountability and living an amoral life. He related the significance of these cruelties to the proclivity of nature to bare her wrath without warning. He held a tight grip on the customs of Old China, but dangled precariously on the edge of a changing society.

The fear gripping his community was palpable, and Zhao Shu was also racked with despair. Should the National Army—or worse, the Japanese—discover her husband's writings, he would be killed along with his family. At times, she questioned his loyalty to his family; due to his participation in activities considered subversive. These were the only times in her many years of marriage the couple argued. Lady Zhao worried that the love of her life was slipping away.

****

Zhao Heng worked hard to stay the course, moving his studio into his house to be away from the center of town. It was only a matter of time before the Japanese would march into Suzhou, bringing death and destruction.

Instead, out of harm's way, tucked into the edge of the forest, Zhao Heng could continue teaching his students and preparing his son to become the next Master Calligrapher.

Heng felt perplexed by his son. Jian was a strange boy, spending long hours away from home and showing immense disrespect for his art. While the Master's other students labored all day hunched over their writing desks, brush and ink in hand, Jian was scratching at the wood of his desk or staring at the wood planks on the floor. Zhao Heng wondered what made Jian act like he was so hungry that he would devour the entire floor if it were served to him on a platter.

And then there was Ming, who was also growing restless. The siblings were sixteen years old, and Ming was becoming a young woman. She had slipped through puberty, landing inside a delicate body. She exhibited poise and grace. Her face had become thinner and her eyes, wider. Her fingers long and lean—her chest, once boyish, now sported small, round breasts. For a brief moment, Heng imagined Ming as the enviable beauty in the village and the desire of every eligible bachelor. Then, he remembered ....

In the grand homes of the affluent families, aunties spent hours collaborating, spinning webs of love matches around the marriageable girls and boys. A good match was a profitable investment, however, Ming was a liability. Though Zhao Heng could provide a healthy dowry, he could not guarantee that Ming could produce a healthy child.

Zhao Shu had given up on a future for her daughter and failed to take notice when Ming's breasts developed, or that she needed her mother's support when the bleeding began.

When the aunties rounded up the cousins to explain the duties of becoming childbearing wives, Ming was left alone in her room to dream of a marriage that would never happen and to bear her changing body alone with trepidation.

When in town, Ming used her paintings to express her angst and desires as she watched young couples her age flirting. She captured them strolling along the canals dressed in fine wedding attire. She painted the joy of young mothers pushing buggies with their children. She placed all her dreams of happiness into her watercolors.

Jian was acutely aware of his sister's alienation and loneliness. It weighed heavily on his conscience. He had learned from his science and anatomy studies that Ming's deformity was a freak accident of birth, not hereditary, and therefore not predisposed to repeat in subsequent generations. He scoffed at the superstitions whispered by the villagers and argued with his grandparents when they blamed Buddha for their family's misfortune.

At times, he wondered if his mother's small physicality contributed to Ming's abnormal development. Perhaps there just wasn't enough room in Lady Zhao's uterus to carry two babies.

Jian was reminded over and over how active he was in the womb; kicking, poking, and punching during all hours of the day and night. Could it be possible that he was the cause of Ming's misfortune? Did he somehow strangle the blood flow into her right foot, choking the life out of it? These thoughts haunted him more and more with each passing year, and he resolved to help make Ming become a normal, eligible young lady.

****

77

Traditionally, birthdays were celebrated modestly every ten years, except at one month after the birth (to ensure the baby lived), the tenth year, the sixtieth, and every ten years thereafter. Each of those birthdays would be marked with big celebrations. However, Jian decided to honor his sister on their sixteenth year with a special gift.

Jian had spent six years apprenticing in Mr. Guo's studio and exhibited so much talent that Master Guo pronounced him the next Master Carver. How Jian wished he could share his passion and this honor with his family. He wanted to bring home his carvings and wished they could be hung in the house for the family to enjoy.

Sadly, that would never happen for the firstborn of a Master Poet. Though he desired to please his father, he found working with the brush clumsy and the ink uncontrollable.

Wood was a different story. Strong and solid, it spoke to him. Inside each block of wood was a soul yearning to be released. The hours spent smoothing the hardness, caressing the curves, tapping and scraping, were entrancing.

When a figure emerged from a block of wood, he felt victorious. He lived for the moment when he would take his first step backward and gaze with awe at the beauty he had created. His carvings were liberating.

****

"Ming, get your coat, we're going for a ride," Jian shouted through her bedroom window.

"Where?"

"You'll see. Just meet me in front."

Ming placed her brush in a cup of dirty water and hopped over to fetch her wool coat lying over the chintz chair in her bedroom. The coat had been worn by an older cousin and given to her for a birthday present.

Ming was amused by the irony of the combination of these two items together. She liked to imagine the reverse was true instead—*I'd rather wear a dress made of French chintz and sit on a wool upholstered chair than wear this itchy, old coat.*

Jian was waiting for her outside. He propped up the bicycle and helped her mount the seat. He had grown taller, an inch more than his father, so the twins could no longer ride the bike together. Ming steadied her weight, applying more pressure from her right leg to balance and keep the bike upright. Jian walked the bike through the village and up a hill to Master Guo's studio.

Once a busy shop filled with the sounds of rasps and chisels pounding and transforming large chunks of ash, cherry, and oak into intricately carved furniture, it had become a hollow cavern. Dusty outlines on the walls and floors, where massive pieces of furniture were built and shipped to grand homes, were the evidence of a once thriving business. Since the Warlord Wars and the invasions of the Japanese, only remnant planks of wood and sawdust littered the concrete floor. Still, the sweet aroma of tree sap hung in the air and played the role of seductress, beckoning Jian's heart.

Reaching the studio, Jian helped Ming off the bike.

"I've got you. Come inside."

"Jian. What is this? You're flushed. Was I too heavy to push up the hill?" she worried.

"Come, dear sister, and see what I have made for you," he smiled.

He swooped her up and carried her inside through the darkened cavern and into a small room located in the back of the studio. On top of a workbench stood an unusual wooden apparatus with metal hinges, leather straps, and brass buckles. The base was concealed by a swath of scarlet silk fabric.

"Jian, did you make me a sculpture?"

"Take off the cloth and you will see."

Ming approached the gadget with caution.

What a mysterious thing, she thought.

Gently she folded the soft fabric in her hand and it slid away to reveal a carved wooden foot.

"Master Guo got a commission to make a *Yu*. I helped him carve the dragon shapes and he let me use the remnants. I made you a foot, Ming. Now you will be whole."

Ming held the contraption in her arms. The wooden foot was a perfect match for her normal foot.

"It's made of birch leaf pear," she marveled.

"Yes, we have an abundance of that in our village. And look, I made a joint so that you can walk, like me," he smiled.

Ming lost her breath. She turned and threw her arms around her brother's neck. "Oh, Jian, I can't believe you made me this beautiful thing!"

"Here, sit on this stool and we'll try it on."

Jian slipped Ming's tiny foot into the socket he'd carved at the base.

"I lined the inside of the foot with fleece, Ming, so it'll feel like a slipper."

He buckled the leather harness around her calf. Steel shanks ran down the sides of her leg and fastened to the ankle of the foot. Ming stared at the device in disbelief.

"Come on, let's give it a try," he urged her.

"How?"

"Stand up. Hold onto me."

When Ming was a little girl, she would steal her Mother's right slipper, pack it solidly with tissue paper, and scoot around her bedroom floor pretending she was an elegant lady, attending the most fashionable social engagements and commanding respect. Those brief moments in her bedroom prison made her feel whole—made her feel normal.

Upright, Ming noticed her left foot was equal in size with the wooden right one. Jian had duplicated her long, slender toes.

Ming felt the pull of Jian's weight against her body. Finally, her dream to walk like a fully formed lady had come true—yet she felt terrified.

"Raise your right knee and bring the foot a little off the ground, I want to make sure it doesn't slip off."

She lifted the device off the floor. The weight pulled on her calf muscle.

"Okay? Are the straps too tight?"

Ming could only shake her head, *no*.

"Good. Now, slowly set the foot down, heel then toe, a little in front of your left foot. And rock your body forward. I've got you. You won't fall."

Ming clung to her brother and took a step.

"Okay? Good. Now bring your left foot up to the right one," he continued.

For the following ten minutes, the siblings inched their way across the carving room. The leather harness rubbed the skin of her leg. They paused while Jian added a fleece liner to prevent chafing. Never had Ming felt more admiration and pride for her brother than at this moment. He was so focused and secure in his world.

Not even a Japanese invasion could disrupt Jian when he is working—Ming mused.

Strapped back in, Ming rose off the stool without her brother's support. "Let me try."

"Wait," Jian ordered. Running over to the worktable he reached for a record album and slid the vinyl disk onto the turntable of a dusty old phonograph. The speakers crackled to the sound of a waltz.

"A foreigner left this album and player for Master Guo. If you walk to me, you and I will dance to celebrate your becoming a whole person."

Knee up, foot out and down, heel first, then toe. Rock the body weight forward and the left foot follows.

"I feel like a baby walking for the first time," Ming whispers.

"Well, you are doing great, Baby. Keep coming. Just a few more steps."

"I hope you are not in a hurry to get somewhere."

"No, Ming. Here is where I was rushing."

The wooden foot slapped down onto the floor. The sound echoed off the walls.

"Easy, I worked hard on that thing. Don't break it on its maiden voyage."

"Oh, sorry," she laughed nervously.

Two more steps and she faced her brother. With her arms outstretched, he helped her get into a waltz position.

"It's okay, I've got you. Rest your hand on my shoulder. When I step forward, you step back, then rise up onto the balls of your feet. Don't worry, the hinge at the ankle will bend. Follow me to the side, then step forward and now, to the other side."

Ming felt her body become rigid and tight.

"Try to relax, Ming. You are as stiff as that plank over there. Try to feel the music. Hear the rhythm? One, two, three, one, two, three. Feel it?"

Ming paused. "Yes, I feel it. I'm sorry I'm so clunky. I keep stepping sideways and I don't want us to trip and fall."

"It's okay, Ming. Waltzing will help you get your balance and get used to the joint on the foot. Ready?"

She nodded, *yes*, determined to master this challenge. Again, she held her right hand high, rested the left on top of his shoulder, and stepped forward. In time, she was able to relax her body and put her trust in her brother and his magical creation.

Together they traversed the carving room and danced into the empty studio space. The tinny sound of musical notes reverberated off the bare walls. Each phrase prodded her to take the steps that made her confidence grow and her movements smoother.

Jian matched his sister's smile. Ming was a whole person now, and he had righted the wrong that had been his curse for sixteen years. They were dancing together, two normal siblings—laughing and marking circles in the sawdust.

Chapter Thirteen

Jian could count on one hand the times he saw the look of satisfaction in his father's eyes. The evening he brought Ming into the house, wearing her new foot, was one.

Lady Zhao wept with joy at the sight of her daughter standing on her own in the middle of the living room. Hearing the commotion, Zhao Heng left his studio to join his family. He knelt down to examine the device wrapped around Ming's calf, studying the eloquently carved jointed foot attached at the bottom.

Ming proudly announced that the designer who crafted her new right foot was her wonderful twin brother. She raised her leg so that her father could have a closer view. Zhao Heng examined the bolts, hinges, ball joint, and leather harness that defined the device.

"Look Baba! Jian even matched my skin color. He made me pretty toes," she laughed.

"Yes, I can see that, Ming. That is quite an engineering feat. Show me how it works."

Ming took a few steps towards her mother and threw out her arms. Lady Zhao met her daughter with a warm embrace. Zhao Heng placed his hand on his son's shoulder and whispered, "Wonderful," as he walked out of the room.

For the next two years, Ming mastered the task of maneuvering around her home and garden with her prosthetic foot. She and Jian would take long walks, and he would challenge her by placing obstacles in her path. Ming counted the hours until their studies would be finished and Jian would get a break from the writing. Those days were the happiest. The horrors afflicting her country seemed to bypass her world.

Ming and Jian spent their free time walking, fishing, singing, dancing, and laughing.

Jian continued to make improvements to the device. When Ming had a small but noticeable growth spurt, Jian fashioned a new foot to match the size of her real one. Ming proudly displayed the original carved foot on a shelf next to her paintings.

Though Jian and the foot brought her a sense of normalcy, it was the bicycle that gave her freedom. Learning to ride was the top priority on her list of everyday activities to master. Jian spent most of his spare time helping her accomplish that goal. It wasn't long after that wonderful day, when "The Skaters Waltz" echoed throughout Mr. Guo's dusty woodshop, that Ming was able to move about her village—on her own.

****

Ming shivers. It isn't the darkening sky threatening a storm or the uncertainty of the fate of her village bringing on the chill. It is a much larger concern. Jian—her protector and confidant—had grown distant and defiant over the past year.

They are eighteen years old, and he is feeling multiple pressures. There are the openly discussed marriage possibilities, friction over their father's impatience, and anxiety over the threats of invasions.

Ming can't soothe the turmoil in Jian's heart. She has tried to get him to talk about it, but he changes the subject—or worse—makes excuses to cancel their time together that she cherishes. She wishes he could be released from the burdens of being the firstborn son. If only her father allowed Jian to pursue the artistry that makes her brother so special.

The chill of his pain makes her stop the bike and pull at her coat. She knows he is running from Baba, from his anxiety of disappointing his family, and from his anger, frustration, and sadness.

On the day of an impending monsoon, when strong winds would kick up the sea and flood the village, she feels instead Jian's wrath. Ming knows what he is running from—and where he is running to.

At the edge of the village, Ming lays the bicycle against a tree and follows Jian into the woods. At first he is furious to be discovered, but watching Ming navigate the thick forest floor, using the prosthetic foot he crafted, softens his heart and so, Ming is invited into his secret world.

Part Four
Yuanfen

Chapter Fourteen
The Trans-Siberian Railway

Day 2

Dear Elana,

I hope you are doing well and are able to pass the time happily with the family. I have to admit the days are long and the nights even longer. Sometimes I join in a game of cards with the other travelers in the dining car.

The people have been very kind, and many of them call me Rabbi, which would make Papa laugh. It looks like I'll be asked to lead a Shabbat service when Friday evening arrives.

I know it is wrong to mislead, but it seems my presence gives the Jewish people on the train some comfort, so

I don't have the heart to correct them. Plus, since my ticket only affords me one meal a day, the people have been generous, sharing with me the extra food that they pick up during our many stops.

I share a decent cabin with a family of four in the second-class section. The father insists I sleep on one of the two upper berths, the two little ones share one bed, and the parents sleep on the bench seats.

I pass the time reading and entertaining the children with stories and drawings. They especially enjoy hearing about all our naughty times with Levi. For them, this is all one big exciting adventure, but I feel the trepidation in the hearts of the adult travelers.

We are now labeled refugees. How did this happen? How did one group of people manage to displace thousands so easily?

Elana, looking out my window I'm seeing endless fields of ice stepping up to the horizon. Miles and miles of birch trees rise up to touch the white sky. Where do these fields of ice lead? I'm thinking that they are a metaphor for our future. We are stranded and homeless and will, again, live our lives wandering lost in this vast emptiness, like Moses in the Sinai.

Even though I am surrounded by ice and snow, in my head, all I see is the yellow, orange, and grey of the fires that burned inside the synagogue. I'm very worried about the Torahs. Did any of them survive?

I do have a surprise for Akiva, which will make him very happy. I am carrying the little Torah he calls the "Baby," wrapped around my waist. The bulk is heavy and hot, but I dare not share a word about my secret with anyone, as I must deliver this Torah to Papa's new yeshiva in Kyoto.

I can't tell you how anxious I am to resume my work. Once in a while, when the family is away, and I am alone in the cabin, I take out my quill and run the feather through my fingers. The smell of the carbon powder takes me back to my attic studio.

I can feel the stiffness of the parchment as it crackles beneath my hand and the rush in my heart as the ink flows from my pen. I miss the golden light that pours through my narrow window in the afternoon.

This Siberian light is harsh, cold, bluish grey—a light of dread. Ah, excuse my being morose. What gives me comfort is knowing that when I look out the window, you were looking at the same scenery one day prior. I'm glad we are traveling down the same path.

Yours truly, Moshe

****

Day 3

Dear Elana,

I am saving my letters to give to you when we are all together. It's strange to think that we no longer have an address for our mail to arrive. Do you think our mailman is still making deliveries to houses where

91

there are no families to receive letters? Do you think the Germans will be able to extract Mr. Bernstein from his chair at the post office? I hope you are finding my sentiment amusing.

The men on the train spend much of the day and night drinking vodka. I can't say I like the taste of it, but I'm as bored as they are, and the alcohol relaxes my itchy fingers.

I'm longing to write, and I miss working. I doubt I'll ever retire. One day you will discover I have passed away with my body slumped over a Torah scroll. I dare you to try prying my quill from my death grip.

The family that I'm sharing a cabin with is very friendly. Mr. Brodsky is a very studious man. He taught astronomy at the university in Vilna. He likes to challenge me to debate the existence of life from the scientific perspective versus the religious teachings.

I believe he enjoys our little sword fights, lobbing ideas, facts, and ideologies back and forth. And while neither of us could ever win this debate, we do enjoy calling a truce over a glass of beer. He is a spirited man who is dedicated to teaching his students. I can tell that he is suffering inside the same as I.

We are currently sitting on a sidetrack waiting for the westbound train to go by. These hour-long stops give me the opportunity to stretch my legs. I took a walk around Ekaterinburg and stopped by an old cathedral. Nearby is a wooden cross marking the site where Tsar Nicholas II and his family were executed.

Maybe it was the icy cold of the day, or the remains

of the vodka circulating through my veins, but I suddenly felt a sense of paranoia. The royal family was brought to this city on the Trans-Siberian railway, and shortly I will be rejoining my travel companions on another trip to nowhere.

I wish you were here, Elana. I know you would pull me out of my malaise. Without my family and my friends around me, I feel as though I left for school but forgot my books.

Yours Truly, Moshe

****

Day 4

Dear Elana,

It is close to midnight, but I cannot sleep. Today, Russian soldiers boarded the train when we pulled into Krasnoyarsk. We were told to stay in our cabins, or our seats, and then the soldiers came in and made every passenger give up their jewelry, watches, and belongings of value. When I heard that they were coming closer, I grabbed my sterling silver yad, remember it? It was Papa's gift to me for my bar mitzvah. I slipped it into the coat pocket of Mr. Brodsky's little daughter.

The soldiers were gruff, and their demeanor frightened the children. Mr. Brodsky took off his watch and handed it to the soldier. Mrs. Brodsky cried as she removed her wedding ring. One soldier grabbed it from her hand and slipped it into his jacket pocket. I will never forget the grin on his face as he taunted the poor woman.

Then they shouted at me in Russian, but I didn't understand what they were saying. They gestured for me to stand up and ordered me to turn around several times. The two of them pointed and laughed.

They ordered me to spin faster. I knew they were making fun of me, but I caught the fear in the children's eyes and decided to find joy in the humiliation. I threw up my arms and twirled, pulling down suitcases from the overhead storage, bouncing into the bunks and flinging dishes and leftover meals to the floor.

The children shrieked with laughter and joined me, spinning around our cramped space. Even the guards got caught up in the silliness and spun their way out of the cabin. They laughed and said the word "clown," in English.

I told myself that it was I who had the last laugh. Whatever names they were calling me had no impact on someone who doesn't understand Russian. So, if that's the worst they do to me, then so be it. But Elana, it wasn't the worst.

Soon after they left we were allowed to get off the train. I offered to take the children for a walk, maybe to find some candy. The children held onto me tightly as we walked around the station and out onto the platform. Just as we were about to board, the soldiers returned and grabbed Mr. Brodsky.

Mrs. Brodsky was screaming and pleading as they took him away. I stood back with the children and as the soldiers passed me, Mr. Brodsky, looked into my eyes. I felt the chill of fear.

Mrs. Brodsky pulled on one soldier's arms and he pushed her down onto the pavement. As they walked away, one of the soldiers turned and looked at me. He made circles with his finger and laughed again, mocking me, "Funny clown!"

The children cried themselves to sleep, and I am at a loss as to how to console Mrs. Brodsky. She is understandably distraught and at one point yelled at me about God deserting her and her children. Papa would know what to say, he would have the words; his voice would calm her. I know this to be true because I've watched as people just as upset as Mrs. Brodsky fall to his feet in despair.

Papa's way of soothing desperate souls is a gift that I did not inherit. My words come easily with ink and quill, but fail me in voice.

I'm grateful you weren't here to see this cruelty. You probably would have gotten arrested for punching the soldier in the stomach. I have to stop writing this letter because my head is throbbing. It helps to lean my forehead against the window glass and let the chill from outside soothe my pain.

Yours Truly, Moshe

****

Day 5

Dear Elana,

There is much confusion amongst the passengers about the location of our final destination. I heard that the Japanese have changed their minds about allowing more refugees to enter Kobe. They have exceeded their quota and are now redirecting us to Shanghai, China.

Many people are worried. They have heard that living conditions are terrible there, that the people are hungry, that sewage flows into the streets. There is a very brutal Japanese sergeant who proclaimed himself "The King of the Jews," who rules over the Jewish people in a ghetto. Can you imagine that? Well, he can call himself whatever he chooses, but we answer to one and only one Supreme Being—and he's not Japanese!

I don't trust the information I'm hearing about the Japanese plans for us, so I am going to switch trains and make my way to Beijing. There, I've been told, I will be able to find someone who, for a fee, will bring me to Shanghai.

Baruch Hashem—I pray that He guides me back to you.

Yours Truly, Moshe

Chapter Fifteen
Suzhou, China

The stench of fish blankets the air wafting over the crowds at the Suzhou Railway Station. The fishmonger warns, "Buy your fish quickly now! The storm is coming, be prepared. Buy fresh fish now!"

In the early morning of the sixth day since he left his home, Moshe steps onto the platform at the small railway station in Suzhou, China. His plan to arrive in Beijing that evening changed when the train pulled into the Suzhou station, and it was announced that traveling by rail would be suspended until the storm passed.

The anxiety of the crowd rushing onto the platform is palpable. A strange electrical sensation charges the air from a thunderstorm looming in the distance. A wall of deep grey marches over the horizon; this will not be a typical rainstorm. Something big is coming and Moshe knows that he must find shelter.

****

Muddy water sloshes up the banks of the canals that lace through the old section of the city. The rich fusion of colors turns to stone grey. Moshe squints his eyes against the harshness of the stark light. Walking along Pingjiang Road, he passes empty shops. Gusts of wind blow open the door of Master Zhao's studio.

Moshe steps inside and closes the door.

He calls out, "Hello?" But no one answers. He removes his hat and places it on the chair next to a writing table. A breeze teases the wind chimes that hang outside the window.

Moshe sits and takes a moment to gather his thoughts and the tears flow. Alone in a foreign country, in a stranger's shop, he is overwhelmed with a loneliness that paralyzes his soul. Exhaustion overtakes his body and his stomach churns with hunger.

Looking around the room, he notices evidence of a hasty departure. In one corner, a rice cooker, still plugged into the wall, spits out water. A *wok* with leftover vegetables sits on a hot plate. Moshe helps himself to the food, and though the vegetables are soggy and the rice burnt, he is grateful for the meal.

Lightning flashes and a large clap of thunder shake the building. The electricity goes out, leaving Moshe in the dark. In a back room, he discovers an antique hurricane lantern.

He laughs at the irony—*Good for the Maccabees, good for me. Kenahora, I won't still be here in eight days.*

Holding the lantern up Moshe notices the hangings that grace the walls around the room. Long narrow strips of rice paper flutter softly in the draft, seeping through the windowsills. The bold vertical lettering is curious. Shining the light onto the wall, he examines one of the banners.

Master Zhao's writing table contains a work in progress. Moshe wipes his hands on his woolen coat and touches the paper. It curls around his hand. He holds the paper against the lantern glass. Diffused shadows dance around the flame. The structure of the paper, lightweight and thin, is the antithesis of the stiff, cumbersome parchment he uses for his Torah writing. The rice paper catches the draft and floats above his hand.

Moshe reaches into his satchel for his writing box and retrieves the quill. Dipping it into the bowl filled with black paint, he writes the name, *Amalak*, then scratches it out. The tip of his quill tears the paper and the paint seeps into a blot. The paper disintegrates and disappears.

Moshe rubs his hands together; the chill in the air does not dampen his interest in this discovery. He studies the characters resting on the paper; strong—yet delicate, angry—yet shy, quiet—yet chaotic.

He recognizes this artistry. This work is by the hand of a master. Holding the paper horizontally, at eye level, he studies the depth of the ink imbedded into the paper. For portions of the characters, strokes of paint rest lightly upon the surface. With others, the paint seeps deeper, clutching mightily to every fiber.

Moshe's long, slim fingers wrap around the handle of a watercolor brush resting in a porcelain vase. He dips the toe of the brush carefully into the bowl of paint and takes a breath. Over a week and many miles have passed since he held his pen in his hand. His heart pulses in his chest. He studies the silhouette of a character. The configuration is different from Hebrew, but the application appears to be the same.

Resting his hand onto the paper, he flicks the tip of the brush, making his first stroke. The paint lies down lightly.

Twisting the wrist allows more concentration of ink and a heavier flow. A flipping motion adds a slight curl up at the tail of the letter. Resting the brush sideways produces a beveled edge.

The distances between the lines appear to be critical to the meaning of the character. Moshe's strokes are deliberate and measured. His first attempts prove awkward, and he lets his mistakes slip down to the floor.

The lamplight reflects off a small puddle of water forming on the tile floor. Moshe goes into the little room in the rear of the shop and returns with a few towels. He stuffs them under the door.

Perhaps God brought me here to be guardian of this work.

****

Sheets of rain pour down onto the village. Lightning and thunder rattle windows and rooftops. The wind roars through the trees, causing the pontoons to crash against their moorings.

In Master Zhao's shop, Moshe hears only the characters speaking to him. This strange combination of dark and light strokes must have significance, and he relates to the strength and beauty living inside each figure. He holds the paper gently, so as not to leave fingerprints on top of the surface. Lightly he flicks at the brush, copying the outline of the finished work. Twisting the handle, he lays down the paint, working on the beveled edging. He swims in a river of symbols; characters that tell stories hidden within their borders.

This strange writing deserves Moshe's full respect, and it is important that he honor this master's work. He focuses on the distance between the lines and the variances of the shapes. He is aware of the spacing between each of the letters. Within an hour, he replicates the characters on the scroll that was left behind on Master Zhao's desk. He steps away to compare the two samples.

Moshe is flush with exhilaration. For the first time in many days, he feels truly at peace, alone in this studio surrounded by the work of a great artist. This place in time—this moment—is a blessing. He will work through the storm and guard the work in the event of flooding. He will spend the night studying, practicing, and following the path forged by this Master Calligrapher.

Chapter Sixteen

For three days and nights, fierce winds batter the village. Outside the studio, a thick wall of water pours down from the sky. Moshe dutifully wrings the wet towels into a bucket and secures them under the front door and along the windowsills. There will be no end to the flooding.

He is grateful that inside he is warm and content; no soldiers to taunt and senselessly frighten him, no train ride filled with endless boredom. In this sanctuary, surrounded by beauty, he is at peace.

Focusing on the layout of the work is particularly interesting, especially the vertical structure occupying long sheets of paper cut into narrow widths. Moshe hopes that soon he will meet the Master artist and discover the significance of this work. He places the watercolor brush into the cup of dirty water and sits down on the sofa against the wall.

It is the third night of endless rain.

How did Noah tolerate forty days and nights?

Mental and physical exhaustion are overwhelming. He lays his head upon a satin lined pillow and instantly slips into a deep, peaceful sleep.

****

Far in the distance a woman's voice is screeching. The language is unfamiliar and incomprehensible, and the pitch; extraordinarily high. Rising from his stupor, Moshe becomes aware that perhaps he isn't dreaming—or alone in the room

"Aieee. Get out! Get out!" screams Lady Zhao.

Moshe stirs from his haze. Then, *whack.* Rough bristles scratch his face. Lady Zhao stands over the sleeping figure on her husband's sofa, screaming—

"Get out, Devil! Go away!" Thwack. She wields a broom, hitting him across his shoulders as he jumps up.

Sensing fear and anger in the woman's voice, Moshe responds calmly. "Okay, okay, Ma'am, I'm not here to hurt you."

Lady Zhao finds this intruder's language, along with his imposing physique, equally peculiar. She studies his long, knotted hair and rumpled dark clothing, then raises her broom. Neither understands each other's language as they speak rapidly over each other.

"Please, stop hitting me. I'm not here to do any harm!" Moshe pleads.

"Devil! Out! You will not curse the house of Zhao!!!"

Whack. Hit. Smack. Moshe jumps away from the blows.

Lady Zhao's screams bring a crowd of shopkeepers to her door. Moshe runs through the group, knocking his hat to the floor. The villagers chase after him shouting, wielding their sticks, umbrellas and brooms.

"Get the Devil!!!"

"Run him out of town!"

"Curse the storm that blew you to Suzhou!" they shout.

Moshe runs down to the canal and over the bridge, past the shops, and into a residential neighborhood. Still the crowd pursues, pelting him with rocks and shouting in high-pitched voices that are foreign to his ears.

At the edge of the village, on the banks of the Yangtze River, the crowd stops. A wall of people stands in silence, transfixed on the *Devil*. Moshe takes a step in their direction and, in unison, the crowd steps back.

102

What did I do wrong? What's wrong with these people?

"Hello?" he calls to them.

Lady Zhao raises her broom and yells, *"Go away, Devil. Go far away from Suzhou!"*

Moshe can tell by her tone that he is not a welcomed visitor. He will need to find his way back to the railway station and continue his journey to Shanghai, but getting back to the center of town will be a challenge. He will have to wait until the crowd disperses. He turns towards the riverbank as the crowd heads back to their shops.

****

Zhao Heng is anxious to have life return to normal. He is relieved but surprised that his studio escaped the damage that the storm inflicted on his neighbor's shops. Surely Buddha has blessed him. He wipes the mud off his boots and begins setting out the paints, papers, and brushes in anticipation for the return of his students. Over on his writing desk he notices a dinner plate. Remnants of rice stick onto the surface, and a brush is resting in a bowl of murky water.

This is strange. I would never leave a brush in dirty water. It will get ruined! Such laziness is intolerable.

Zhao Heng's attention is diverted to a sheet of rice paper lying on his desk. It is a replication of the poem he was writing prior his hasty evacuation. Zhao Heng adjusts his bifocals while comparing the brushstrokes on the two sheets of rice paper.

He places one of the sheets against the window glass. Sunlight halos the character on the paper. Instantly he recognizes the perfection of each individual stroke. He notices an identical banner on the wall hanging next to his—*How curious? How could this possibly be? I was the last to leave before the storm.*

The villagers reach the front door of Zhao Heng's studio. Breathlessly they speak over each other, boasting how they successfully chased away the Devil who was lurking evilly in his shop.

"Master Zhao! You should have seen him!"

"The Devil of Darkness, in your shop!"

"We chased him!"

"He's gone!"

"He fell in the river and was swept away!"

"A curse on him!"

"We may be powerless against the Orientals, but against a darker power, we are victorious!"

"You would be proud of me, husband," Lady Zhao says as she steps through the crowd and into the shop. "I found him sleeping there." She points to the sofa.

Zhao Heng leans down and picks up the hat lying on the floor. He is familiar with the Old World style. The tag on the fedora reads, *Borsalino.*

"This hat was made in Italy. It belongs to a foreigner, and not *any* foreigner, a devout, religious man." He looks at the paper in his hand and his heart quickens.

"This is an educated man. He is like me with his brush. He is *not* the Devil. This man is a Jew! You must go find him!"

"What?!?" Lady Zhao yells, stunned by her husband's order.

Zhao Heng turns to the crowd. "Find this man. Bring him to me. We should be ashamed at our disrespect. We must ask for forgiveness. Now go! Find this man and bring him back here. Quickly!"

The crowd turns in unison and heads in the direction of the river.

****

It had been two weeks since Moshe jumped out of the comfort of a warm bath and into a state of chaos. Sitting by the edge of the river, he dips his hands into the cool water and splashes his face. He feels grimy,

104

and the bulk of the parchment wrapped around his waist is hot and itches. He removes his boots and lets the water wash over his feet. The rush of the river drowns out the shouting in the distance.

Stooping over to clean off the mud on his boots, Moshe becomes aware of a presence lining the bank above. The crowd of people has returned, shouting and raising their sticks, brooms, and umbrellas—*These people are crazy!*

Moshe grabs his boots and takes off running, the crowd following above. The weight around his waist slows his pace, and the footing is precarious. He slips and his body flies forward. He slides along the rock bed—bashing his head against a boulder—and his body goes limp. The crowd stops and stares down at the foreigner lying still beside the river.

"Is he dead?" one merchant wonders.

"Husband, husband!" Lady Zhao shouts.

Zhao Heng pushes his way to the front of the crowd. He turns to the grocer, "Go back and get your vegetable cart! We'll bring him to the House of Zhao!"

The village men climb down to Moshe's motionless body. Blood oozes from his scalp and mixes with the dirty water.

"He's knocked out but breathing!" The merchant yells up to Master Zhao.

The men struggle to haul Moshe up the embankment. They lay him down at the feet of the Master poet.

"You will see, my wife, that the storm has brought us an important guest. We must make him comfortable in our home. Go ahead, and prepare the staff for our arrival. And have Jian fetch the doctor."

Lady Zhao nods, for whatever displeasure she is feeling at this moment must be endured silently. Social norms dictate that welcoming a strange foreigner into her home would not be proper. However, the years spent living as the Master's wife have confirmed that her husband would never jeopardize the welfare of his family. She will trust that bringing this stranger into her home has a purpose, and that the mysteries of his appearance in her village will, in time, be revealed.

Chapter Seventeen

Ming couldn't remember the last time the House of Zhao played host to a visitor. One of Baba's students had arrived ahead of the crowd with the news of a foreigner in an accident.

"Master Zhao says to tell the maids to get a room ready for an important guest!"

A rush of cool air catches in her lungs. Maids flutter through the house carrying piles of freshly laundered linens. Cook starts a large pot of soup on the stove, and Jian arrives with the doctor. When the cart pulls up in front of the grand home, the villagers carefully lift Moshe and carry him inside.

Ming steps into the shadow of the foyer and watches as they struggle with the body. Zhao Heng enters barking orders, warning the men to take great care. Lady Zhao brushes past Ming without a glance and disappears down a staircase leading to the kitchen. The men stumble under the weight of the stranger.

Ming finds the visitor's appearance vulgar; the tattered black garments, his beard caked with dried blood. He emits a foul odor that hangs in the air.

"Don't be afraid, Ming," Zhao Heng calls to her. "This gentleman is just unconscious. He should awaken soon."

"But Baba, why did you bring him here?"

"This injury is our fault," he admits. "This is a learned man, Ming. We must help him. It will be an honor to have him as a guest in our home."

"Yes, Baba," she resigns, holding her scarf to her nose.

The village men settle Moshe onto a bed in the guest room on the first floor. Master Heng sends all the women out of the room so that the doctor can begin his examination.

"There is a nasty hematoma measuring approximately two centimeters on this man's forehead and a deep wound above his ear," says the doctor. "I will need a bowl of hot water and some clean rags. I'll have to stitch this gash."

Zhao Heng turns to one of his students. "Go to the kitchen and have Cook give you what the doctor needs." He motions to one of the villagers. "Help me remove this gentleman's overcoat."

Lying prone on the bed, Moshe looks to be a robust man. The men slip off Moshe's heavy woolen coat and his dress shirt. It is the undershirt with the tassels attached at the corners that are the most puzzling to the villagers.

"Baba? What is the foreigner wearing?" Jian asks.

"This man is a Jew, Jian, his clothing is part of his religious practices. Go ahead, take it off but be careful. We need to have him bathed and his clothing cleaned before he wakes."

Call it serendipity—or fate—that washed over the House of Zhao that day. Zhao Heng will forever be grateful for the raging storm that forced a young scholar, a fellow Master of the Calligraphy Arts, to seek shelter in his humble studio on Pingyang Road.

The removal of the stranger's clothing revealed an amazing discovery—a small Torah wrapped around the waist of a learned man. Though the majority of Master Zhao's life had been dedicated to the study of ancient Chinese writing and poetry, occasionally his curiosity led him to read about the writings of different cultures, especially the Aramaic and

Hebrew writings contained in the Sacred Scrolls of the Jewish people. However, he'd never had an opportunity to see a Torah—until now.

Immediately he recognized the bundle of wrapped parchment and understood the significance of its long journey to Suzhou. It took over twenty minutes for his students to carefully uncoil the Torah wound around the waist of the foreigner.

Searching the pockets of the woolen overcoat, Jian retrieves a wooden box containing a feather quill and a pot of dry powder for ink. He also discovers the silver *yad*. Holding it gently in his hand, he marvels at the engravings carved into the silver along the stem.

"Look, Baba, this stranger is a writer too. And what is this silver thing?" he asks. He studies the *yad* in the window light.

"I believe it is used for reading the words in this Torah."

"It looks very old."

"It must be very special. It has been on a long journey." He watches the students unrolling the little Torah and smiles. "Careful," he instructs, "do not let the oils from your hands touch the parchment." Jian is aware that this moment is having a profound affect on his father. Master Zhao turns to his son. *"Yuanfen,"* the father whispers.

"Yuanfen," the son repeats, with doubt.

****

A quiet reverence settles over the household on the evening of the foreigner's arrival. Zhao Heng takes his meal in his studio on the ground floor. He wants to stay close by should the sleeping man awaken. Earlier that day, Ming watched her father leave the guest room cradling a bundle in his arms. He disappeared into his private studio and failed to join the family for dinner.

"What a waste," Lady Zhao sniffs, glaring at the uneaten fish lying on the silver platter. No one at the table speaks, for their normal jovial banter might disturb their special guest. Perhaps he will sleep through the night and then, in the morning, Ming will learn his name and homeland. Lady Zhao finishes her meal and retires to her bedroom.

Jian picks at his food. Today he had to forgo spending time at Master Cho's woodshop. He was in the process of completing a carving for a wealthy client, and Master Cho had promised to share the payment if the work could be delivered today. Now, with the sudden appearance of this mysterious man, everything has changed.

"I don't like this," Jian says, pushing his food around his plate.

"The foreigner?" Ming asks.

"He ruined everything. I didn't finish my work. Now Master Cho won't pay me. I curse the wind that blew him here!"

"Where do you think he came from, Jian?"

"Don't know. Somewhere in Europe, probably."

"How did he get to Suzhou?"

"How would I know? Why do you care?" His bad moods have grown more frequent over the year.

"What's wrong, Jian? Why are you so grumpy?"

"I don't like having a stranger in our house, Ming. Did you see Baba? He thinks he's had some divine intervention from Buddha, but Mama still thinks he's a devil. The man smelled bad, and he ruined my day. I'm going for a walk. Call me if the Son of Abraham rises from the dead."

Jian pushes back his chair, leaving Ming alone at the table. In the distance, the voices of the maid's laughter penetrate the silence. Their cacophony is shrill and irritating. Ming heads to the guest room.

"What is so funny?" Ming whispers from the doorway.

The maids jump quickly from the bedside and gaze at the floor. Periodically, they catch each other's eyes and giggle.

"Tell me what is so funny?" Ming commands.

One of the maids speaks. "Sorry, Mistress, it's—it's his ..."

"Yes ... his what?"

The second girl blurts out, "His *yin jing*."

The girls giggle.

"Not like a sausage," says one, covering her mouth with her hand.

"What?!" Ming gasps.

"It looks funny. Not like the men of China," says the other.

"Go! Leave now," Ming demands.

Gathering up the bathing bowls and the wet towels, the maids hurry out of the room. Ming carries a lit hurricane lamp to the bedside, watching the stranger breathe deeply. When he was brought into her house she thought him to be an old beggar man. Now he has been shaved and bathed.

He could be my age, she thinks. *What are these strange sideburns?*

She leans in closer to check his breathing. Being alone with the foreigner is oddly thrilling. She studies his features: the crook of his nose, the strong chin, the soft curve of his earlobes, the pasty color of his skin. He is a mystery.

Ming listens for the silence in the room, then gently lifts the sheet to take a peek. Suddenly Moshe grabs the sheet to cover his body, and Ming falls backward. He jerks his body upright in the bed. Her long braid whips him in the face.

"What? What is happening?" Moshe yells in Polish. He looks down at the girl crumpled on the floor.

"What? What are you saying?" Ming answers in Mandarin.

They stare at each other for a moment.

What an odd creature—petite, pale, with black hair and eyes.

"Where are you from?" Ming asks.

He doesn't answer. For once she is happy to have studied geography.

"Are you from *Francaise? España?*"

Moshe shakes his head, no.

"How about *Deutschland? Italia?*"

Why is this girl listing countries?

"*Россия?* United States of America?"

"America!" Moshe lights up. "My brother lives there! Do you know America?" Moshe asks in English.

"My brother too," Ming answers, also in English.

"He does? Where does he live?"

"Upstairs."

"What?"

"I know what you are saying. I have brothers too," Ming smiles, proud of herself for finding a common language. "I am learning to speak in English. Hello. I'm pleased to meet you. How are you on this very fine day? I have two sisters. Your mother is pretty. Do you like music?"

"I'm sorry, Miss, but I don't understand you." Moshe winces in pain.

"English!" she laughs. "You understand English. We are having friendly talk. Did you learn English in school?"

"Yes, but—" Moshe's head is spinning.

"Tutor taught us," Ming says excitedly. "Baba says we need to know English if we want to stay ahead in commerce. Tutor taught me that commerce is a fancy word for business.

"English has a lot of that, right? Like the word right and write. It sounds the same, but not the same meaning. So confusing, right? The one spelled with an "r"—the other a "w." My manners are forgotten. Are you thirsty? I drink you."

"I guess. You speak very well." Moshe touches the bandage wrapped around his head. He winces with pain and wishes the girl would stop talking. "Maybe whisper?"

"Thank you. Yes, I know how to whisper." She lowers her volume, "I know over a thousand words. I can whisper them to you if you'd like. Tutor says I am an English Master, but Baba pays him to say that. Hey, that's commerce, right?" she brightens. "I say a joke!"

Moshe nods, politely.

"You hit your head. Do you hurt?" Ming asks.

"I don't know. My brain is foggy. Where am I?"

"You were brought to my home, the House of Zhao, in the village of Suzhou. What is your name?"

She pulls herself upright, landing close to his face. He adjusts his eyes and Ming pulls back. The lantern illuminates her features. He studies the shape of her eyes and the braids of her dark hair framing her delicate face.

She smiles shyly and slides the fake foot behind her normal one. His gaze makes her blush.

He smiles. "I'm Moshe Lozinsky, from Vilna."

"Vilna is your home? I know that Vilna is the capital of Lithuania, Mr. Lozin ...."

"Moshe."

"Mr. Moshe." Ming looks down.

"Just Moshe. You seem to know a lot about countries," Moshe smiles.

"Yes, geography is my favorite subject. One day I hope to visit every capital." Realizing she should not be having a conversation with a stranger, she backs away. "Please excuse me. I should not be disturbing you."

"No wait, what is your name?"

"Zhao Ming-Hua, from Suzhou," she adds shyly.

"I'm sorry," he says, steadying his head. "I didn't catch that."

"Catch? Like with ball? I didn't throw anything," she laughs.

"No, I mean I didn't understand your name."

"Oh, you can call me Ming. It will be easier on your crazy brain."

Moshe smiles and rests his hands upon the covers at his waist. He rises quickly. "My Torah!"

He panics, patting down the empty space. "What have you done with it?!"

"I'll get Baba!"

"Baba?"

"My father, he has your ... Torah!"

"Okay yes, good. Please get your father!"

In her haste to leave the room, Ming's foot smacks against the hardwood floors. The thumping matches the pounding in Moshe's chest. He pulls his body out of the bed to stand. The room begins to spin and he slips back into darkness.

Chapter Eighteen

For three days, Moshe surrenders to the hospitality of the Zhao family. Ice packs cool the swelling from the gash to his forehead; rice dishes and soups warm his belly. Periodically, he receives visits from the family, who are kind and welcoming.

Every day, Master Zhao brings the Torah for Moshe to hold. It is a relief to know that his host treats the little Torah with sincerest respect.

Zhao Heng anticipates the day when Moshe will be well and join him in the studio. It will be refreshing to have the companionship of a fellow scribe, especially one whose penmanship he admires. With the master's mounting interest in Moshe, Jian is mostly ignored. The distraction brings both relief and distrust, as Jian doubts the integrity of this stranger.

****

A crisp breeze teases the branches of the trees surrounding the garden. The fall season brings new games for the village children. Talks of impending invasions inhabit the conversations of the villagers. None of this is of any consequence to Zhao Heng. He tunes out the children's laughter and the chatter. In spite of the chill, he has set up his writing table under the pagoda in the center of the garden.

Ming brings out a woolen blanket, places it around his shoulders, and sets up her easel nearby.

Moshe puts on his coat and joins them outside. He underestimated his physical condition when he arrived at the Zhao's and still feels weak and unsteady.

"I hope I am not inconveniencing you, Master Zhao."

"Ah, my friend, not in the least. You must stay until you are well enough to travel. Come sit. Join me."

"Your garden is magical. I wish my mother could be here to see it. She would cry with joy."

"You are a close family?"

"Very. My youngest brother and two sisters are with my parents. They were supposed to go to Kyoto, but I heard they were sent to Shanghai instead. I was on my way to find them when the storm hit. My eldest brother lives in America."

"Really? Well, soon you shall be reunited," Zhao Heng says and points to a passage in the little Torah lying open on his writing table. "In the meantime, tell me about the artifacts at the top of these letters. I am curious of their significance."

Moshe stretches to see where Zhao Heng is pointing. "Um, that is a *nun*."

"A *nun*?" Master Zhao repeats.

"Yes. Traditionally people think the letter looks like a snake."

"And this mark at the top?" Master Zhao points.

"I form a crown at the top, signifying that all Jews can become kings if they dedicate their lives to learning and living Torah."

"Ah yes, very majestic. Come sit. Write with me."

Moshe nods to Ming and then joins the Master Poet. He slides a brush between his fingers.

"Follow my movements," Zhao Heng says, guiding his brush through

116

the air.

Ming smiles at her father.

"You see?" he continues. "Twist your wrist and flick the brush. Turn your hand slightly inward towards the ground."

Moshe follows the Master's movements.

"Now repeat, only faster. Impulsive. Push through the movement—you get restraint, the uneven balance of the lines—rebelliousness. You attain elegance with the fluid strokes. Emotions are conveyed through the physical application."

"Yes, I see. I understand."

"Good. Now dip your brush in the paint pot and copy this character." The Master slides a sheet of rice paper to Moshe, who studies the single character on the page. He dips the brush and steadies his hand against the paper. The ink flows too quickly.

"Try pivoting your hand outward slightly," Zhao Heng instructs. "Remember, the amount of pressure implies the meaning of each character."

Moshe takes a new sheet of rice paper and reaches towards the inkpot.

"I'll try again."

"Wait," says Zhao Heng, "allow your brush to almost run out of ink before refilling."

Ming smiles to herself. This stranger, so revered by her father, has now become his pupil.

"What are you working on, Master Zhao?"

"Ming, will you translate?" he asks his daughter. "Her English is better than mine. I'm not certain if you will understand the meanings."

Ming follows, lending voice to his poetry—

"*Center your boat down the river, for you will get stuck too close to the shore.*
Keep to the forest path, for you will wander forever in darkness.
Your steps have brought you to the path's beginning.
Will you walk them again?
The dragon awaits."

Ming smiles at her father.

"Fascinating," says Moshe.

Zhao Heng nods. "This character here represents the common man. These lines are of a life out of balance with nature. This character here is the peace we strive to obtain. This one represents the dragon that stands in the shadows and threatens our choices. And this character ... is the mistake we continue to relive."

"That is a subject my father reminds us about many times," Ming says with amusement. "His poems are filled with metaphors."

"It is my desire that my poems awaken the intellect and search for higher meaning."

Moshe laughs, "My father would agree with you. He teaches from the Torah, which is filled with allegorical stories, parables, and metaphors. He also—"

Master Zhao interrupts, "Your father is a learned man?"

"Yes, he is a renowned Rabbi, well known even outside of Lithuania."

"Ah, I see. Are you studying to become a Rabbi like your father?"

"Oh no, I am a scholar. I prefer to surround myself with parchment and ink, not teaching at the *yeshivah* or listening to the troubles of our village."

"Of course. It is the eldest brother who honors your father by becoming a religious man."

"No, not Levi either. He left the old ways behind to live a more modern life. He never liked the constriction of our old ways."

Zhao Heng sighs. "Then your brother Levi leaves your father's heart in pieces."

Ming looks up from her painting. Moshe studies the Master, hunched over his writing table.

"With respect, Master Zhao, my father understands that Levi's need to follow a different path doesn't diminish his reverence or honor.

"Our *Kidushin* teaches us that—*'Revering means not standing in his place, not sitting in his seat, not contradicting his words, and not overpowering him; honoring means providing food and drink, clothing and covering, taking out and bringing in.'* Levi would lay down his life for our father, but he isn't expected to be him."

Zhao Heng returns to his calligraphy, embarrassed that he pushed his opinions onto a stranger.

Moshe smiles at Ming, who clearly enjoys this moment. He looks over at her painting.

"Now that's something I never had a talent for. May I see?"

The scene on the canvas is early fall, a sprinkling of green clings to the boughs of the trees while children jump in the piles of fiery leaves below.

"That's very beautiful, Ming. I hope one day to own one of your paintings."

Ming blushes.

The Master stirs his brush into his water pot and sighs, "Picasso once said, *'Had I been born Chinese, I would have been a calligrapher, not a painter.'*"

Chapter Nineteen

Beneath the stone bridge that spans the canal over Pingjiang Road, Jian huddles with a group of his father's students. They lower their voices when villagers pass by. One dressed in a Zhongshan suit playfully places an army cap onto Jian's head.

Nearby, Ming rides the bike while keeping a sharp eye on her brother. Lately, Jian has been acting aloof, preferring to spend his time going to meetings with his friends than with the family.

Moshe joins Ming and nods towards the group of young men.

"What's going on over there?" he asks.

"I don't know, but I don't like it. I'm afraid Jian will get into terrible trouble. Baba hates the Communists and would never allow Jian to join their movement. Jian is easy to impress and lately he's been acting distant. He echoes their ideas. It scares me."

The chill of her words hangs in the air. Moshe thinks of his countryman who followed the rants of a delusional voice and rose up in blindness to the destruction of their homeland.

He attempts to cheer her up.

"You ride your bike very well, Ming. I'm impressed."

Ming steers the rusty bike in circles. "You mean because of my foot?"

"I guess, but you are making me dizzy. How about staying by my side while I walk?"

She keeps to his pace, thinking about her riding. "What does your magic scroll say about people born like me?"

"You mean the Torah?"

"Yes, the Torah. I can't be the only person in your history born with a deformity."

Moshe watches a flock of birds soar over the canal. "That is a complicated question, Ming."

"I thought so," Ming says, catching Moshe's hesitation.

"The Torah states that no offspring with a defect shall be qualified to offer the food of his God, meaning he can't assume a leadership role."

"So, like me, a broken person is solely fit for the life of a beggar," she sighs.

"But the great thing about these texts, Ming, is that they are not absolute."

"What do you mean—absolute?"

"Not the final rule. In this case, at the time this was written, it could have pertained to needing people to be physically able-bodied to pull their weight. Our Talmud also teaches—*'Do not look at the container, but what is in it.'* We are taught to see each other as whole, sacred human beings.

"You are an artist, Ming. The importance of your talent must not be underrated. I, and every other human being, have no right to judge your character based on your physical nature."

Ming considers his words.

"While I consider my foot a challenge, I never forget the luck of my birth." She adds, "I have parents and siblings who are my champions, even though I know my mother and aunties worry that I could destroy their gene pool.

"Still, I am grateful. I follow the guidance of Chuang Tzu, an ancient poet who said, *'Flow with whatever may happen, and let your mind be free. Stay centered by accepting whatever you are doing. This is the ultimate.'*

"So, I paint, I study, I experiment, and I look for truth and meaning in my life. One day I hope to be recognized as one of the great painters in the world."

"Ah, I like that," Moshe smiles. "And may I add, *'Treat no one lightly and think nothing is useless, for everyone has a moment and everything has a place.'* You will find your place Ming, no doubt in my mind."

The two travel down the road, away from the village. The sounds of the crowds in the streets grow distant. Moshe relishes the serenity of the trees and the water, while Ming rides alongside basking in the warmth of her new friendship.

"Moshe, does that mean in your village a person born like me could be a leader?"

"Well, I wish that could be the case."

"See?" she says, suddenly defiant. "What is the term? I know—hypocrite!"

"No, not because of your foot, Ming, it's because you are a girl. But you are right. I bet if Elana was allowed to be the leader of the world she'd find a way to stop this lunacy that is going on in our countries."

"Is Elana your sister?"

"No, my school friend," Moshe softens. Saying her name affects a pang of melancholy and loneliness which weighs heavily.

Ming steers the bike towards the pathway leading into the forest.

"Follow me. I will take you somewhere special."

****

The thick canopy overhead blocks the light along the forest path. Moshe hesitates, staring into the darkness. Ming leans her bike against a tree and slips her hand into his. His mind spins. Touching a young woman is forbidden. The Rabbis would disapprove, but the forest is ominous and the darkness up ahead, unnerving.

For almost a mile, Moshe depends on Ming to guide him through the dark; their footfalls sink into the moss. Large stone boulders jut out from the dense forest ground as the two climb above the tree line.

"Is this a quarry?" Moshe asks.

"Shhh. Soon you will see," she answers.

The path takes a steep incline. In spite of the burden of her wooden foot, Ming springs up the hill like a deer.

As Moshe catches up, he sees Ming standing on top of a boulder above and recalls the dream he had of Elana.

"Ming, back up! Don't stand so close to the edge!" Moshe warns, but Ming laughs, kicking some pebbles over the ledge, raining down onto his face.

On the plateau, Ming motions to Moshe to crouch beside her. He follows her gaze down to a ravine below, where life-size wooden carvings cling to the steep granite walls. Powerful birdlike creatures perch among the boulders, four-foot tall wooden flowers spring from the rocky soil, a fisherman is at war with his catch, a dragon's fiery breath guards the ravine from strangers.

"What is this place?" Moshe asks.

"Suzhou."

"Suzhou? We are in Suzhou."

"Suzhou Jian," Ming whispers.

"Suzhou Jian," he repeats. "This is amazing."

"Shhh," she says, grabbing his hand and squatting lower. Her eyes reveal a sense of mischief. Moshe feels a tug in his chest; his heart beats faster. His hand melts into hers and he can't stop smiling.

Down below, deep into the crevasse, Jian moves into sight. He drops to his knees and focuses on carving a design on the surface of a wooden creature. Moshe reaches into his pocket and pulls out the crumpled paper airplane he had made for Akiva a few days before they left their home. Straightening the wings, he cocks back his arm and lets it fly.

Swiftly, the paper plane glides above the ravine—circling overhead—until losing altitude, dropping at the feet of the young Master Carver. Jian snatches the airplane, looks up, and waves them away.

"Ah," Ming sighs. "What a grump. Come on, I'll give you a tour."

Ignoring her brother, Ming leads Moshe down the steep path to the opening of the ravine. The carved dragon guarding the entrance eyes Moshe with a fierceness that stops his heart. The two weave through a maze of sculptures, stopping in front of the life-sized fisherman who sits alone without a catch.

"The full moon churns the sea," Ming recites. *"Winds howl and cry. Fisherman will go hungry tonight."*

Moshe slides his hand along the surface of a Lotus leaf.

"Ah, the festival tonight," Ming continues. *"For the snow has left the earth. We shall rise with the sun. The Lotus is showing its splendor."*

He stops in front of several crouching figures and Ming's voice whispers in his ear— *"The lake rests softly upon the shore. Boughs kiss the ground. Sit beside the water. Be still."*

Moshe turns his attention once again to the dragon. Ming places her hand upon the dragon's head—*"Center your boat down the river, for you will get stuck too close to the shore.*

Keep to the forest path, for you will wander forever in darkness.

Your steps have brought you to the path's beginning.

Will you walk them again?

The dragon awaits."

"Ah," Moshe realizes, "you are reciting Master Zhao's poems. Represented in carvings!"

Ming answers, "That is right, Moshe."

"Jian?"

Ming nods. Moshe moves closer to the crouching artist. "But Jian, when did you sculpt all this?"

Jian ignores the question and walks to the opposite end of the grotto.

"Over many years," Ming continues. "Whenever Jian could escape his studies, Master Cho let him take remnant wood pieces and tools for carving."

"Magnificent. What your father must feel about this honor to his work!"

"Oh no, this is a secret. Our parents must not know. Suzhou Jian is our secret and now—yours."

"But they would be so proud of Jian!" Moshe argues.

"I'm afraid that is your wish only."

Moshe admires the workmanship and the minute detailing. He wanders the ravine tracing every curve, feeling the sharp angles, touching the intricate design patterns in the woods. "Everything is perfect. Your dragon reminds me of the two-headed creature that guarded the ark in my synagogue in Vilna. Jian, you are a genius."

Jian scowls, but Ming intercedes. She is annoyed by her brother's rudeness.

"I think so and so does Master Cho, our Master Carver. But ..."

"Master Cho is not your father. I understand," Moshe sighs.

"Yes," she nods. "I would never want Jian not to be my brother, but I sometimes wish that he was born to Lady Cho, not Lady Zhao. You are our friend, Moshe, promise me that you will honor Suzhou Jian and not give away our secret."

"Yes, of course," Moshe says as he takes in the wonder of this magical place. He watches Jian skillfully carve decorative scales into the side of a fish. Suzhou Jian has been a world lovingly nurtured and guarded for many years, but it has become an unfortunate burden on the shoulders of an extraordinary artist.

Chapter Twenty

In the farthest corner of Zhao Heng's home studio, Moshe sets up his writing desk. The table is smaller than the one he used in his attic room in Vilna, so the little Torah hangs off the edge and rests on a stool. Today's work is a disappointment.

Since arriving in Suzhou, progress with the Torah writing has been slow. He stares at a letter etched into the parchment where the ink has cracked. A smudge spills over where the lines should be pristine. No letters may touch so, incredibly, Moshe has made an error.

The muscles in his neck tighten. He rubs the knot in the back of his right shoulder blade as he shifts his weight on the little wooden stool.

You are mocking me, little letter? he sighs. Zhao Heng looks up from his rice paper.

"Something troubling you, Moshe?"

"Sadly, I made a mistake."

"Can it be repaired?"

"Yes, I can scrape it off."

"Here," Zhao Heng says, offering a tin filled with razor blades.

"No, no, Master Zhao, nothing metal can touch the parchment. I need to use a piece of glass."

Zhao Heng turns to his son who, as usual, is distracted from his work.

"Jian, go to Cook and bring Moshe some glass. I'm sure he has some. I've heard much crashing in the kitchen of late."

"Yes, Baba," Jian says, but rising from his desk, a pamphlet falls to the floor—*Strategic Problems of China's Revolutionary War by Mao Zedong.*

Zhao Heng stares at the pamphlet title. His look switches to fury and disappointment. Jian snatches the pamphlet and backs out of the room.

"Ach, communist propaganda!" Zhao Heng spits. "This Mao is—how you say—cut from the same cloth like that worn on the shoulders of Adolf Hitler."

He rubs his face. "I despair, Moshe. I fear for our children's future. They don't see that this Mao wants to rob their souls and turn them into robots. I am losing my son."

Moshe looks at the great poet, now seemingly frail. "I have faith that if tested, you will find that not to be true," Moshe says.

"You have more faith than I," the Master sighs, resuming his work. "Tell me, Moshe, why do you write?"

"To be closer to God and to preserve our heritage. I believe God wants me to take this journey with pen and ink, not weapons."

"I believe my journey is to wake up my people," the Master says. "Encourage them to raise their voices, not lie around silently waiting to die."

"Lady Zhao," Moshe says, "has mentioned that she is afraid that you are inciting violence with your poems."

Master Zhao nods. "Lady Zhao lives in a world with many fences. It's my fault, really. She is my jewel, and I have worked very hard to ensure her world is safe and joyful. But, outside our beautiful garden awaits a harsh world.

"China has more than one enemy here. Yes, there are the Orientals who wish to rule our country, but within our community many are following leaders who have selfish motives.

"They are the power grabbers. I fear that even if they were to succeed at running the Japanese off our land, these young communists would unwittingly turn this country to totalitarianism. We would be no better off than the poor Germans who are being led astray by the unspeakable sickness of a few.

"I am too old to fight in the battles to preserve our beloved country, but I can strive for freedom through my poems. And, I admit that I am selfish. I love my life. I love that my hard work and dedication to my art affords my beautiful home and garden, that my wife is happy and my children healthy and educated."

Zhao Heng looks at Moshe. "That is my truth, my poems, my voice," he says, dipping his brush into his inkpot. "Are you not concerned with what will happen to your world if all the educated people are chased away? Do you understand that you are compromising your future by not using your gift to speak out?"

Moshe remembers, "That was one of the last discussions I had with my father. Apparently, Hitler thinks the educated Jews are taking up space that, in his opinion, should be occupied by German intellectuals and scientists—thus inhibiting future advancements. If he was smart, he'd realize that the section of the German population who make up the scientists, doctors, inventors, and writers, *are* the Jews."

"That is very true, so write that."

"I've never been political, Master Zhao."

"Yes, but deep in your heart, Moshe, what are your beliefs?"

"What do you mean?"

"What is important to you? What would it take for you to pick up your quill?" says the Master, offering up a challenge. "When—how do you say—your back is up against the wall?"

"That is not hard to answer, Master Zhao. I strive to live an honest, religious life and follow the Commandments."

"I find that troubling." Master Zhao rubs his eyes.

"How so?" Moshe sets down his quill.

"I fear the deafness of people. It is true that society needs structure for peaceful cohabitation. But I worry that blindly following the dictates of one ideology will lead the flock away from obtaining a healthy spiritual existence. You are aware of the horrors being inflicted upon your people, are you not? Your writings are your legacy. Your breath is in every

129

word—your blood inhabits the ink."

"Thoughtful words to be sure, Master Zhao."

The Master holds up a blank sheet of paper. "Consider this, young scribe. A blank sheet is a life fractured. Are you not compelled to speak about what is in your heart? Are you afraid that if you exercise free will you would be punished by your God for being a deviant?"

Moshe bristles at the thought. "I guess you could argue that my free will is the choice whether or not to comply with the laws of Torah. And lately, I have been wrestling between my religious responsibilities and my circumstances, which are in violation of my beliefs."

"What do you think your father would say on this matter?"

"My father never had to face extinction until now. I wish he was here to offer his insight and speak with you on this matter."

"I would be most interested. Perhaps he would have words for Jian. Perhaps he would succeed with my son where I have failed."

"Yes, Master Zhao, you are correct that my writing serves a different purpose than yours. I alone cannot stop the atrocities happening today. All I can do, at this time, is survive and make sure this Torah survives. I am a chosen guardian of the work created by my ancestors.

"If the Jewish people were to become extinct, somewhere, someone in the future will have a record of our existence. Someone will let future generations know that we lived as spiritual people—full of faults, yes, strong in will, respectful of nature—that we thrived, and we loved. My truth, Master Zhao, can be summed up in one word—*preservation.*

"You are writing as a means to express your concerns about the existence of your people. I write to prove that my people lived. Outside these walls, my fear is insurmountable. Inside, today, in your home, I'm in control of my life and my craft. Each stroke is committed to memory. The execution, taught to me by my elders. I even control the mistakes I make, and today I realize that I have lost my focus."

Zhao Heng studies the young scholar. "I see you are very committed to your work, Moshe. Your father would be proud."

Slowly, methodically, the two dedicated writers resume their work—Moshe's pen scratching the surface of parchment—Zhao Heng's brush flowing silently across paper made from rice. Two souls—separated in purpose and culture—united by the artistry of the written word.

****

On his way back from the kitchen, Jian stops in the doorway of his sister's bedroom. Ming sits curled up in the alcove, sketching the winter garden.

"How could you do that, Sister?"

"Do what, Jian?"

"Suzhou Jian. How could you give away our secret?"

"Jian, you act like Moshe is the enemy, an evil diety."

"He is, Sister. He is a foreigner."

"What is wrong, Jian? I like Moshe. What I don't like is you these days. You are changing and I'm worried."

Jian is both hurt and resolved. "China is changing, Ming. You are young, yet you are fighting what is destined to happen. You are behaving like Baba, holding on with your fingernails to a vanishing life. Mark my words—get on board or be left behind."

"You are scaring me, Jian," she says, holding her hands out to him. "I am afraid of these words you are saying. Please Jian, promise me you will never turn your back on your family."

Jian doesn't go to her; keeping to the doorway he looks to the floor and shakes his head.

"Jian?"

He looks up. His eyes bore holes into hers. "Be careful, Ming—be careful of your friendship with the Jew."

****

Jian returns to the studio with a jar filled with chipped pieces of glass. He resumes his place at his writing desk, avoiding the judging looks from the man he reveres and fears.

Moshe sets to task, scraping the ink off the parchment. Zhao Heng raises the paper up to the light, content with the characters imbedded within.

"Ah, I am happy with this banner. Jian, I want you to place this in the studio window."

Jian looks at his father with concern as he reads the inscription. "Eyes looking East—see not the western bird—yet, hears the anguished cries." Jian returns to his seat.

"I think not, Baba."

"What? You are ashamed of my work, Jian?"

"Yes Baba, your words will unleash the anger of many and bring harm to our family."

Master Zhao's eyes fill with rage while Jian remains resolute.

"Excuse me, Jian," Moshe interrupts, "but I don't believe your father would ever put his family in jeopardy."

"What do you know? How can you speak? Why are you here? This is the house of Zhao, not a *yeshiva*. You are not welcome here!" Jian hisses.

Moshe recoils, embarrassed. He would never take advantage of the family's hospitality. Perhaps he has overstayed his welcome.

"Hush, Jian!" Zhao Heng yells. "You will not speak to our guest that way!"

Jian grunts and goes back to his lesson.

Moshe blows the dust off a scrap of parchment and readies his quill; he writes the name *Amalek*, and then crosses it out.

"Moshe, please explain. I've noticed this ritual you perform prior to each writing session," the Master observes.

"When the Jews escaped from slavery in Egypt," Moshe answers, "the leader—Moses— had his soldiers take the position at the head of the group to protect the people. The older people, the infirmed, and the mothers with young children were positioned in the rear for safety.

"The *Amalek* were a cruel tribe who attacked the Jews from the rear, killing and injuring the ones who were defenseless. Traditionally, *sofers* like myself write the name, *Amalek*, on a piece of scrap paper and cross it out to blot out the evil. Then, I am safe to begin my work."

"I see. Maybe I should try your ritual. I will write the name Mao, then cross it out!" the Master muses.

"Hush, Baba!" Jian scolds. "Talk like that will get you arrested."

"Nonsense. I am not afraid of those hoodlums."

"Oh no, Baba?" says Jian. "You should be afraid, and grateful."

"Grateful?" The Master looks up at his son.

"Yes, Baba. Why do you think your garden was spared from total devastation during the invasion two years ago?"

The Master knits his eyebrows together. "What is this you are saying?" he asks.

Jian pauses, then answers. "You are Master Zhao, the Great Poet of China, the most revered living writer for our homeland. No matter what you think about the ideologies of the young revolutionaries, they hold you in high esteem. They, along with the army, did everything they could to keep the enemy from advancing their campaign this far from town. Your neighbors near the south were not so fortunate."

Moshe watches the great man steady himself as Jian continues, "Baba, your mind is stuck in old China, but we are being invaded now. Our people are hungry. The Communist Party is gaining strength. You have to face the fact that the revolution is coming. The rebels are fighting the Japanese in the countryside and at the same time capturing the land from the tyrannical landlords—claiming it in the name of the poor people and the youth. See Baba, there won't be beggars in the streets. Everyone will be employed; every child will have schooling. And, no one will go hungry!"

Master Zhao takes a breath, calming himself. "You are swallowing the food they are feeding you, Jian. These words that spew out of your mouth come from a sick stomach. This revolution, as you describe it, is a war against our traditional values. When books, art, and music are controlled by the government, people starve!"

"Our old way of life isn't prevalent anymore, Baba! The Eighteenth Army Group is strong. Would you rather live under the tyranny of the Orientals?"

"Tell me, Jian, do you want to lose your home, be told what to eat and when to eat it? You barely have the patience to practice your calligraphy. How are you going to tolerate long days doing field work?"

Jian explodes, "Maybe I would like a different way of life!"

"Maybe?" Zhao asks. "Your Mao is an opportunist, Jian. I can see him preying on the poor and the uneducated, the farmers, and the field hands. He feeds them his proletarian ideology by promising them the moon. He's taking advantage of China's weakness at this time when we are losing our efforts to combat the Japanese!"

Moshe leans forward, searching for the words that would restore harmony as the tension grows between father and son, but the words fail him.

"But we are miserable, Baba! We are struggling!" Jian implores, "I see our lives getting worse! If you told the truth, you'd admit that you too are unhappy. What is so bad about defeating our enemy and then dividing the spoils amongst all people of China equally so that everyone will have a home and food and clothing?"

"That's a nice dream, Jian, but history shows that no society has lived peacefully in total equality. There is always corruption where the leaders rule, and abuse is inflicted upon the subservient that are forced to do the dirty work. You watch and see whose hands are really dirty!"

"I don't believe Mao would turn his back on us!"

"Us? Not us, Jian, rather you, me, Ming, your mother, and your little brother and sisters will be the ones that will be stripped of our land and money, our spirit, unless—I am willing to *fund* the cause. Then they would gladly make an exception to their supposed doctrine and treat us as royalty."

Jian sits back onto his stool and studies his work. His twisted characters defy the rules of perfection and wrench his gut.

"He's using you, son," the Master sighs. "You and all of your generation. You will see that if he takes over our homeland, he'll become just another *bourgeois* elitist!"

Jian stands, his blood draining from his face. "No, Baba! You are too old to understand! You are stuck in a life that is over. Old China is dead and will never exist again!"

The Master rises. "Jian, please!"

"If you don't wake up and join the Party, you will be left out, or worse!" He turns to leave. "I have a meeting. Please tell Mama that I'll be skipping dinner. I'll eat when I get home."

"Jian, wait!" Zhao Heng yells.

Jian slides out the door. Zhao Heng slumps down onto his stool. "Ai, Jian," the Master sighs. "Lowly fisherman, hooking a whale on a perch hook. That Red Devil has ruined the brains of our youth, Moshe—he has stolen their souls."

"I pray, Master Zhao, that the storm of your differences will clear, and you two will make amends."

Zhao Heng blows gently onto his rice paper and places his brush into the water pot. He draws in a slow breath—essences of garlic and sesame oil rise from the kitchen.

"It is that time," he says, sniffing the aroma filling the study.

"Yes," Moshe agrees, "I was afraid my talking stomach would be a distraction."

"Ah, good, you have an appetite tonight. Lady Zhao has instructed Cook to prepare a special meal in your honor."

"Me? Why is that?"

"Tonight is your Sabbath, right?"

Moshe looks out the window at the sun setting.

"Is it Friday already? I've lost track of the days."

"Yes," Zhao Heng agrees, "that will happen when you are in survival mode. Come, Lady Zhao wishes to have you show her how to light your *Shabbot* candles."

"It will be my honor," Moshe says, securing the Torah for the night.

Chapter Twenty-One

Moshe pauses in the doorway of the dining room. Red and golden cranes adorn the rims of the fine bone china place settings. Crystal goblets and silver utensils shimmer in the light of the setting sun. For the first time since he was forced to leave his family's home, a dinner table is dressed for *Shabbat.* He is at once overwhelmed with joy and heartache.

"Thank you," he whispers, nodding to the mistress.

The family takes their places at the table. Moshe is invited to sit at the place of honor next to Master Zhao.

"Please join us," Lady Zhao beckons. "Will you show me how to light the candles like your mother?"

Moshe retrieves a doily from the buffet and points to the top of her head. "We can make do with this as a head covering, if you don't mind."

"Of course," she smiles.

The young children stifle their giggles under Lady Zhao's steely glare. She places the doily on top of her head, stands before the silver candlesticks, and then strikes a match. The wicks sizzle from the heat of the flame as she lights the candles. "What should I do now?" she asks.

"Circle your hands above the flame three times, then cover your eyes."

Her delicate hands fan the air; the flames dance in the breeze.

"Follow my words," Moshe instructs her.

She nods.

"*Baruch ata Adonai,*" he begins.

"*Ba ... Bar ... uch ... ata ... Ah ... donai,*" she repeats.

"*Elohanu melach ha'olam,*" he continues.

"*Elo ... elo ...* I'm sorry?"

"No, no, Lady Zhao, you are doing fine, there is no hurry. Say, *elohanu.*"

"*Elohanu,*" she follows.

"*Melach.*"

"*Melach,*" she repeats.

"*Ha-olam.*"

"*Ha-olam.* Oh my, this is a little harder than I thought. Please Moshe, you may continue."

"Well, this is an unusual circumstance, but I'm sure it will be okay if I take over."

Moshe finishes the prayer over the candle lighting and then takes his place at the table.

Lady Zhao had Cook prepare a feast starting with a course of *dim sum.* Though not traditionally served for dinners, Lady Zhao wanted to show off some of Cook's specialty dishes.

Platters fill up the spaces in the center of the table: steamed vegetable dumplings with two dipping sauces, meatballs baked in orange peel cups, sweet jasmine rice, chicken feet marinated in a black bean sauce, *jiǎozi, guōtiē,* wonton soup, and two platters of barbecued fish, freshly caught that morning.

Lady Zhao admires the table.

"Nothing has pork, Moshe," she adds. "I know your mother would be very angry with me if I served her son pork on his Sabbath."

Moshe smiles politely. He doesn't want to ruin her enthusiasm with the admission that none of the meal is Kosher and therefore should not be eaten at all. Instead, he is comforted knowing that his papa would counsel him to never step on the foot of kindness—so he will eat the meal.

"What comes next, Moshe?" asks Ming.

"We say the prayer over the bread and wine. Uh, but since I don't see a loaf of bread ...."

"Oh dear," sighs Lady Zhao.

"No, no, it's fine," he says looking around the table. "I think this will do."

Steam rises from the plump round *bao* nestled in the palm of Moshe's hand. Ming giggles.

Moshe recites the prayer for the bread and then raises a cup of wine.

"Baruch ata Adonai, elohanu melach ha'olam, borei p'ri hagaphin.

"Thank you, Lady Zhao. I am honored to have this privilege of celebrating my Sabbath with your gracious family. After all, *Shabbat* is really about resting and enjoying the company of your loved ones. I am grateful for your warm welcome towards me at a most unexpected time. And now, everyone enjoy this beautiful dinner."

"Tell me, Moshe," asks Master Zhao, "would your father be reading from your Torah this evening?"

"He will read tomorrow in the morning. And then, he and his students will have lively discussions. They do argue a lot, but I know my father doesn't feel useful if he isn't pushing his students to exercise their brain muscles."

"Ah, well, your father and I have that in common," the Master laughs, looking at his youngest children. The little ones squirm in their chairs. "What will your father be discussing tomorrow?"

"Let's see, since it is fall, we are somewhere around the beginning of our story. Yes, a story from Genesis."

"Please, Moshe, tell us one!" Ming asks.

"Shh, Daughter!" Lady Zhao scolds.

"No, it would be an honor. Hmm ... okay, here's a nice one. A story of finding love."

"Goodness," says Lady Zhao. "How refreshing. Please, go on."

"Well," Moshe begins, "Abraham, who was blessed by God and chosen as the father of the Jewish people, was very old. He had recently lost his wife, Sarah, and felt it was time to find a wife for their son Isaac.

Since he did not know how long he would live, he summoned his trusted servant and made him swear that he would take on the task of finding Isaac a wife."

"Why couldn't Isaac pick his own wife? I'm sure there were plenty of women in his village to choose from," Ming asks.

"Abraham did not want his son choosing a Canaanite woman from their village, but rather a girl who came from the country of his birth; a maiden from his own clan. And, he did not want his son leaving him because he needed Isaac to take over as a leader of his people after his death."

"But how would the servant know who the right woman for Isaac would be?" one of the children asks.

"Well, Abraham trusted that God would send an angel, which would be a sign, and that the servant would recognize the right young woman as a suitable wife for Isaac. Thus, fulfilling his promise to his Master."

"And if the girl refused?" asks Ming.

"Ah, Abraham was a fair man. If the girl did not want to leave her home, then the servant was free of his commitment."

"Please, Moshe continue. I want to know what happened to Issac." Lady Zhao says.

"Okay," Moshe smiles back. "So, the young man gathered the Master's camels and gifts and went to the city of Nahor in Mesopotamia. Here is where the servant had a thought—*I will make the camels kneel down by the well outside the city. In the evening the women come to the well to draw water. I will ask, 'Please let down your jar that I may drink.' And the young woman who says, 'Drink, and I will water your camels,' will be the chosen wife for my Master's son.*"

"Ah, smart man," says Zhao Heng.

"How is that so, Baba?" asks one of younger children.

"Moshe will explain. Go on, Moshe," instructs Master Zhao.

"Well, not too long after the servant's prayer to God, a young, pretty maiden appeared with a jar on her shoulder. Her name was Rebekah and she was related to Abraham's brother.

"The servant ran to her and asked, 'Please give me a little water to drink from your jar.' She set down her jar and gave the man a drink. Then she said, 'I will draw water for your camels until they have finished drinking.'

"And so she took many trips to the well, ensuring that the camels were no longer thirsty. The servant knew this was the sign he had prayed for. He asked Rebekah if he and his men could spend the night at her father's house. He gave Rebekah a golden ring and two gold bracelets, all worth a costly price. At her home, the servant and his men were offered food and drink—much like you have, Lady Zhao."

The Mistress blushes as Moshe continues, "And a stable and food for the camels. The servant told Rebekah's family about his vow to find a wife for his master's son. He spoke of his love for his kind and fair Master, Abraham, and about how Abraham has been blessed by the Lord and had become a great leader. He obtained flocks, herds, wealth, and servants. Rebekah's brother said that since God had anointed Abraham, then his sister must leave her family and follow the servant to the homeland of his master. The servant insisted on knowing if this decision was agreeable to Rebekah. She must follow of her own free will."

"Oh, my," gasped Ming. "Please, Moshe, what was Rebekah's answer?"

"She said, 'I will go.' The servant gave the family a trove of treasures, jewelry, and garments. The family blessed their daughter and wished her to bear many children. The following morning the servant took Rebekah, along with female servants, on the journey back to the land of Canaan."

"But how did Isaac react when Rebekah arrived?" asked Lady Zhao. "I mean love is more than just time and place. There has to be feeling, yearning, desire. Did Issac feel those things when he met Rebekah?"

"Well, this is where the Lord prevailed. You see, Isaac was meditating in a field when Rebekah rode by on her camel. For a brief instant, they both lifted their eyes towards each other and their hearts joined. So, Isaac took Rebekah for his wife and they had a long and prosperous marriage."

Lady Zhao claps with joy. "Wonderful, I'm so happy for the couple. Perhaps we should ask our servant to find a wife for Jian."

Chapter Twenty-Two

The full moon rises above the pagoda. Moshe tightens the belt around his woolen coat and raises the collar over his ears. As he walks into the garden he is troubled by thoughts of his family. He could never imagine challenging his father in the manner of Jian to Master Zhao.

Somewhere deep in his mind, he remembers a time when a terse conversation between Levi and Papa drifted up the stairs and into the bedroom he shared with his older brother. Moshe didn't understand the words, or why the voices sounded so harsh.

Not long after, Levi left for America and his name was rarely mentioned. At first, Moshe was angry with his brother for leaving him. In time, through the stories written in the letters from America, Moshe found forgiveness. He looked forward to reading about the adventures, discoveries, and new friendships described in Levi's letters. One day, he will visit America and experience Levi's amazing life.

Heading towards the pagoda, Moshe examines the condition of the structure. At one time the edifice was grand and much admired; now sadly, little remains of the gilded paint adorning the carved wooden banisters and arches. Throughout the garden, trees once fruitful stand gnarled, as dormant silhouettes against a colorless sky. Flowering bushes lie in a sickly state of neglect. Fall flowers wilt on the frosty ground.

Since the Japanese arrived, the family has been unable to employ their gardening staff. Many of the workers have joined the National Revolutionary Army or retreated to the safety of their remote villages. Ming looks up from her easel as Moshe steps into the pagoda and sits by her side.

"I'm surprised to find you here, Ming, it's very cold."

"I wanted to paint before going to bed," she answered.

"What is there to paint? All I see are dead tree branches and wilted flowers."

"That's what you see, but I don't."

"Really? Tell me then."

"I will help you see the beauty I see. Come, walk with me." She hobbles out of the pagoda and onto a path lined with weeds and rocks. Ming points to a large elm tree. "Baba's favorite tree," she says. Moshe stops and looks out into the mist at the silhouette. "I bet you see that elm as bare; the branches sharp, cutting through the fog in the night. And, the leaves that are left are filled with holes eaten away by insects."

"Yes," Moshe agrees, "that is how I see the entire garden. In a state of decay."

"Yes, I believe most people would agree with you. Now close your eyes."

"If I do that, how will I see what you want me to see?"

"It's just for a moment, silly. Go on, close your eyes."

With the muscles around his eyes relaxed, Moshe's face settles into quiet serenity. Ming notes the improvement from the strained expression and sickly pallor of the foreigner whose fate brought him to her home only a few weeks ago. She makes a mental note of the crook of his nose, the almost feminine bow of his lips. He looks younger now; just on the cusp of manhood. One day she will paint him, just as he is at this moment.

"Ming, really. Can I open my eyes now?"

"Yes, of course."

"See?" Ming gestures out to the garden. "Look how the moon casts long shadows mixing with the low hanging mist. The light reflects off the bark of the branches making the dark indigo, iridescent. The moon-light shines through the holes in the leaves, casting lacy patterns along the pathways."

"Go on," he says, suddenly interested.

"The garden is bathed in a silvery hue. It's beautiful and invigorating, Moshe. It sparkles, and you only get to enjoy this sight once a month when the moon shines at its fullest."

A gauzy mist encircles her delicate body and shimmers upon her hair. Moshe wrestles with an affection that stirs deep inside; sensations that have been building for Ming since the discovery of Suzhou Jian; feelings that are to blame for restless nights, unable to harness this longing that will not be quenched—*Temptation. Is it evil? If only Levi were here. He would have the words to make this feeling go away. Are these desires unnatural, sinful?*

"Shall we walk?" he offers. The two walk down the pathway observing the patterns emanating from the wilted leaves and petals.

"Are you unhappy here? At the House of Zhao?" Ming asks. "Do you miss your country?"

"I miss my community. When I'm in Vilna, I'm not just Moshe, the *Sofer*. I am a small part of something bigger. I'm a participant in the lives of everyone I cherish. And, every thing too." He smiles.

"Like what?" she asks.

"I'm in the dough baked every Thursday evening for the next night's *Shabbot*. I'm in the heart of every letter sent through Mr. Bernstein's post office. I'm in the heated argument between our two rival jewelers who accuse each other of being color blind.

"And then there is the kindness of Mr. Ravens, who always saves a seat in *shul* for Mr. Polutsky, his best friend—his always late best friend," Moshe laughs. "The great teacher Hillel said, 'If I'm only for myself—who am I?'"

He sighs.

"You said *for* yourself, different than *by* yourself," Ming offers.

"Very clever, Ming." He smiles, then turns thoughtful. "It's just that during this time, I'm struggling to understand the behavior of people. They are forgetting that we are all one species, technically no worse or better than each other.

"I am missing the support of my community who could not only help me feel safe, but help me sort out these questions I have. I am afraid, Ming—what has been happening during my absence? I wish I were feeling stronger and could travel to Shanghai."

She slips her hand into his.

"You need to give yourself time to heal. The trip will be hard." Her slender fingers take on an iridescent hue entwined with his pale complexion.

She whispers, "You can only be where you are now, this moment—us, together as friends, walking in this beautiful garden. You cannot see behind you, and you can only gaze a short distance ahead. Let your heart rest, Moshe."

The time spent traveling through the darkness—landing in a foreign country with customs that confuse, language that hurts the ears, and foods that sicken the gut—led him to a place he'd never expected. A mystical garden. Ming leads him back to the pagoda. His heart wrestles with conflicting loyalties—*I love Elana. I know that to be true. She is my truest friend. One day, kenahora, Elana will be my wife. We will raise our children together. I know that to be true. I love Elana, deeply. I love Elana, yet ... I yearn for Ming.*

"The story you told tonight, Moshe," her voice breaks the silence.

"Yes?" Moshe asks, aware of the chill in the air.

"Will I ever find the love of Rebekah and Isaac?"

She looks at him, sadly. A tear glistens in the corner of her eye and drips down her cheek.

Moshe leans forward, his rough fingers slide against her alabaster skin; her breath moistens his face. Her cheeks blush; her eyes, wistful. He closes his eyes, drinking in the warmth of the moment. She leans into him, their lips part and brush together. Her body presses against his. Her tongue explores the inside of his mouth, featherlike. Her hand rests gently on the back of his neck. Her touch ignites a spark, pulsing throughout his body. He kisses her with a force, swift and desperate. Their passion fuses in a deep, languid embrace. Her body floats above the mist.

Moshe loses himself in an uncharted place. He slows the pace and draws back. A strand of her hair slips through his fingers.

When she lifts her eyelids—she is alone.

Chapter Twenty-Three

Retreating to the alcove in the window of his bedroom, Moshe looks out onto the garden and tries to catch his breath. The pagoda—*Is she still standing there, or did she drift away with the fog?*

The moon has moved on, and he wishes he spent more time with her. Will he ever get his pounding heart back into his chest?

Their kiss was a miracle—a wrong, wonderful miracle. He closes his eyes, longing for Ming, while images of Vilna interrupt his thoughts. The tenderness of her lips, the softness of her skin, the aroma from her hair, imprinted on his fingertips—*What punishment awaits a man for touching a woman who isn't his wife? Wife—Ming? That could never be. Or, could it? Everything about my life has turned upside down. What rules should I follow now, being alone, away from my home? Who is here to judge?*

What if this is now my life? I am the only thing of my past that exists. Is Vilna still standing? I'm here, now, in Suzhou. The rules are changing. There is no Papa in Suzhou, no Vilna, no Akiva, and no Elana. Am I lost or has God led me to this place, to this family? Does he need me to prove my devotion ... to him ... to Torah ... to Elana?

Replaying the moment in the pagoda makes the physical recovery impossible. He remembers how his friends giggled when the Rabbi got to the part in the Talmud that spoke of love and sex. He mutters the words of Rabbi Ammi, "He who excites himself by lustful thoughts will not be allowed to enter into the presence of the Holy One, blessed be He." The rhetoric had been pounded into his brain, but now it is challenging his heart and ravaging his body—*The Mishna states that man does not expend semen to no purpose, yet how will he be rid of this agony? Is this true love for Ming, or purely physical need?*

He slips his hand between his coat and his trousers, falling into the abyss of carnal desire—desperate for release.

****

Aggravation, despair, loneliness, doubt, desire—words flow furiously from his quill. Moshe hunches over his little desk in Master Zhao's home studio, attacking a scrap of rice paper with all the sentiments he is suppressing. The night is still, and he is alone.

What omnipotent being would close a blind eye to the destruction of His adoring people? What God would tear me from my family and force me to live in a strange land with unbearable temptations? Why am I being forced to stand on the precipice of life and death? What God would put me in a position where I'm in love with two women?

His heartbeat slows; the quill in his hand is a comfort. If it turns out that there isn't a "Supreme Being" forcing him to become a stateless person, then perhaps he can find comfort in the writings of his ancestors. After all, the Torah is filled with stories of cruelty and survival, of loss and love. He gathers up the little Torah and presses it against his chest; the voices of the past will guide him; his pain is their pain and their strength will bolster his. He is grateful for their teachings, for as long as he continues inscribing their story—he lives.

Jian walks into the studio, surprised to see Moshe working at this late hour.

"I was hoping Baba would be up."

"No, he went to bed hours ago. I couldn't sleep."

Jian fidgets with the papers on his father's desk.

"Is there something I can do for you?" Moshe offers.

"I doubt it."

"You know, Jian, I've never seen anything more glorious than Suzhou Jian. I believe if you were to bring your unique talent to Vilna, people would stand in line for hours to see your work."

"Ridiculous. You have Master carvers in your own country."

"Of course, there are tradesmen who work at the craft, but what you do comes from a higher place."

Jian stops and sits down facing Moshe. "How do you know that?"

"It's an energy I felt when I stood next to your sculptures. I heard the voices living within the figures."

"That's how I feel when I am standing before a block of wood."

"You can hear the figure inside calling out to you, right?" Moshe asks.

"Exactly."

"Well, the same happens to me. Sometimes the characters fill my head with many conversations."

"You are teasing me," Jian says and starts to walk towards the door.

"Actually, no, I'm not. There are days when I question my sanity. I wonder if the dialogue I'm hearing is imagined or real. Sometimes we argue, and the letters keep me from sleeping at night."

"Yes," he stops and turns back around to face Moshe, "the wood also keeps me up at night. I get no peace until I release my figures from their confinement."

"I'm sitting here at this late hour for the same reason. And as we are speaking, here is one calling to you."

"To me? What do you mean?" Jian leans forward, perplexed.

"Come here, I will show you."

Jian approaches Moshe's writing table with caution.

"Really, Jian," Moshe reproaches, "come closer. I'm not a rabid dog, I don't bite."

Jian takes a tentative step as Moshe dips his quill into the inkpot and braces his hand against the parchment. "Okay, place your hand over mine."

"What, why? No, you are a Jew."

"What? What does that mean? Really, Jian, the blood that runs through both our veins is the same color. I said, 'I don't bite,'" Moshe muses.

Jian eases his hand over Moshe's and around the quill.

"Now, relax your arm," Moshe instructs. "Let me do the guiding."

Slowly, Moshe drags the point of his pen along the surface of the paper. Suddenly Jian's forearm twitches as though an electric current had conducted from the quill, traveling up his arm. He jerks his hand away.

"What! What was that?" Jian gasps.

"Jian, please, be still," Moshe says calmly.

"But I felt something!" Jian insists.

"Please, if I make a mistake, I have to scrape and start again. I can't lift my pen because this letter must be one fluid motion. Understand?"

Jian's eyes open wide, "Yes, yes. Same with my carving." He hesitates.

"Good, you do understand. Now you have to take a leap of faith."

Hand over hand; Moshe guides the ink to form a perfect letter, ד. "It is a *mitzvah,* a good deed which will be rewarded, to write a letter in the Torah, Jian."

"But, I'm not a Jew. Won't that be a problem?"

"Oh, I think if we keep this between us and God, it will be okay."

"What did we write?" Jian's eyes focus on the letter, melting into the parchment.

"The letter is a *dal.* It has several meanings, one being to draw. It's not the pen and ink meaning of the word, but rather "to draw," as in gathering water, pulling inward. There is a word, *deleth,* which means door. Since doors usually open inward, it represents drawing something into your home. You are allowing something, or someone, to come into your life.

"The entrance is a metaphor for being open to a transition, or a way to truth and freedom for the lowly servant. This letter is permanent. It will forever be yours and yours alone. You have now opened a door, Jian. You will be etched permanently in our little Torah. You—and me."

"A *dal,*" Jian admires the letter.

"Yes. Here, I will write it on this scrap of parchment as a souvenir."
Moshe inks the letter and hands the paper to Jian, who places it into the
breast pocket of his uniform. For a brief moment the two young men
share a smile until Jian's posture becomes stiff and he starts to fidget.

"Why do you have to make this your fight, Jian?" Moshe says with a
hint of sadness.

"I don't expect you to understand, Moshe. You were raised in a different world. You come from a gentler people, but look how many of you
are perishing because you weren't prepared to defend yourselves when
evil struck."

Moshe nods. "Yes, Jian, your words are true, but your father's concern for joining the Communist Party and the army has some historical
basis."

"Months ago, before you arrived," Jian continues, "Baba accused me
of being a coward, of having no pride. What was the word he called me?
Oh yes, how can I forget? The word cut me deeply. You may tell Baba
now that finally, I'm no longer *gutless*."

"Fighting an enemy," Moshe argues, "who threatens to strip away
your freedoms is heroic, Jian, but handing over your rights to a ques-
tionable leader *is* gutless. How do you know living under the shadow of
this Mao won't perpetuate social cohesion?"

"Meaning?"

"Meaning, what if Master Zhao is correct in warning that following
this man will rob your souls? What if your entire society begins to speak
the same, think the same, and look the same? What if you are no longer
allowed to practice your art, Jian? I feel for you.

"I'm scared, too, especially because of the passiveness of my people.
We both need to go into our futures with our eyes open. Before you
shut the door on your present, Jian, you need to make amends with your
father. Your father gave you the gift of life and the connection to your
heritage, in spite of your yearning to deny it."

"So, do you go along with everything your father, the Rabbi, stands
for?"

"Of course not. My father, too, is settled in the old ways. Through my
brother Levi, I've learned much about the modern world, and some of
these new ideas are making a lot of sense. I know that Papa would never

153

welcome such changes. I do, however, agree with the teachings that a son must not stand in his father's place."

"Meaning?"

"Meaning, *kavod*—dignity. There is value in honest disagreement, but the manner in which you express yourself is disrespectful to your father's dignity—especially contradicting him in public.

"Your father has fed, clothed, and educated you. He has no expectations of gratitude because it has been his moral responsibility to provide for his children. However, in your case, you have something special. You are cherished, and for that, you carry his heart. There is an interesting story in the Talmud that demonstrates my point, if I may?"

"Yes, of course." Jian's eyes soften as he sits quietly on his writing stool.

"In one passage," Moshe begins, "a son feeds his elderly father succulent food, but when the father asks where the food came from, the son answers, 'Quiet old man. A dog eats quietly, so you eat quietly.'

"In the second passage, a different father and son work the family's grindstone. The King summons all grindstone workers to come to the palace to perform hard labor. The son tells the father that he will take his father's place and that the father will continue his work at home. By doing so, the father will not suffer, or be humiliated, in front of the King. So, I ask you, Jian, which son inherited hell and which inherited paradise?"

Jian fidgets with the piece of parchment in his hand. Moshe rolls up the little Torah and secures the sash. "The ancient Rabbis claim the Torah was written in Black Fire on White Fire. The Black Fire is the words which are permanent and cannot be altered or changed. The White Fire is the spaces around the words. This allows for evolving ideas, imagination, questions, analyzing, and discussion. If I may leave you with a bit of advice?"

Jian raises his eyes to meet Moshe. "You have ingested the Black Fire of Mao. Now, give your attention to the White Fire." Moshe rises and walks out of the room, leaving Jian alone in the quiet of the late evening. Retrieving the paper from his jacket pocket he studies the blot of ink laid onto the scrap of the parchment. The significance of the *dal* is not lost on the young man with a heavy burden.

154

Chapter Twenty-Four

Sleep can be peaceful when the night is calm and void of dreams, but Moshe's body aches and his mind, restless—*Is Ming lying awake in her bed? Does their kiss linger, or will she avoid his eyes in the morning?*

A knock echoes through the hallway outside his bedroom door. Moshe waits until he hears it again. The rap on the front door is urgent, yet no one stirs in the House of Zhao. Moshe walks through the grand foyer and finds one of the Master's students pacing anxiously outside on the porch.

"Hello?" Moshe calls to the student.

"Jian, Jian!" the young man whispers in haste.

"I'm sure he's sleeping," answers Moshe, but the young man doesn't speak English. Moshe pantomimes a sleeping gesture.

"Jian, Jian!!!"

"Okay, come in, I'll get him."

The young man follows Moshe into the grand entry. Moshe climbs the staircase and heads to Jian's bedroom. He knocks on the door and when he doesn't hear any response, peers into the room. The room is cluttered, but the bed is made. Moshe returns and joins the young man who is pacing by the bottom of the stairs.

"No Jian. Not here."

"Jian, Jian!" The student gestures anxiously.

Moshe points upstairs and shakes his head. "I'm sorry, but no Jian." He notes the pained expression on the young man's face. "What is wrong?"

The student flails his arms and runs in place. His words spew out fast, and while the meaning is unclear, the intent is certain—the army is coming to the house, coming to arrest Master Zhao! The visit in the earliest hours of the morning is a warning! The young man rushes out the front door.

Moshe turns and heads down the hallway to Ming's room. He finds her lying peacefully upon her mattress, the covers twisted around her body, her long hair tangled across her face. Moshe lights a lantern and moves closer.

"Ming, Ming," he whispers. "Ming, wake up. Please wake up!"

The girl stirs. She startles.

"It's me, you need to get up!"

"What is it? What's wrong?"

"We had a visitor, one of the Master's students. I think he came to warn Jian that the army is coming for your father."

"Oh!" She rises, grabbing her robe. "Get Jian!"

"He doesn't seem to be here. We need to get your parents out of the house, now!"

Ming hops over to the upholstered chair and secures the prosthetic to her leg.

"Go wake Cook, and tell him to gather some water and supplies. We should head north into the countryside," Ming instructs.

"I've heard that is not safe, Ming. What if we take your family to hide in Suzhou Jian? You could lead us there."

"Oh, no, we couldn't. It would be bad for Jian if we didn't get his permission. He was furious with me for bringing you there."

"The discovery of Suzhou Jian will be a small consequence compared to the anger your father will feel when he discovers that Jian joined the

Eighteenth Army Group. Quick, wake him and your brother and sisters, and I will meet you in the garden."

****

At the foot of the bridge near Pingjiang Road, a group of soldiers gathers. The officer in charge orders the young men to march five miles to the outside of town, to the great House of Zhao. There, they will detain the Great Poet who has been engaging in subversive activity by writing poetry denouncing China's campaign against the Japanese and criticizing the principles of the Chinese Communist Party. The officer calls the small troop to attention when he notices one is missing.

"You!" the officer shouts as he singles out one of his soldiers. "Go and search for your comrade, Zhao Jian. He might have warned his family. Quick!"

Under the cover of the fading moon the soldiers march in formation. They will race the sunrise and secure their mission by silencing the voice that threatened to undermine their cause.

Chapter Twenty-Five

Night sounds exist; some wondrous—melodious choirs of birds, frogs and crickets, yet some are perceived as haunting—torturous echoes of something hunted. Tonight, there are none, only stillness interrupted by the occasional sound of twigs crackling beneath the weight of plodding footfalls.

A snap of dead foliage along the pathway might alert the authorities. Slowly, under a canopy of darkness, Ming leads the family deep into the forest. It had taken Moshe almost fifteen minutes to reposition the little Torah around his waist after he had woken Cook and the staff. There had been no time to grab personal belongings. Servants pull wheel carts hastily packed with supplies.

Moshe and Zhao Heng each carry a sleeping little child as the group walks in silence. Moshe finds hiking through the forest in the darkness laborious under the weight of both the little Torah and a sleeping child. Lady Zhao winces in pain; the nettles grab her ankles and tear her stockings. For a mile, the group pulls the carts over the rocky pathway.

"Up ahead is the start of the mountain trail," Ming whispers.

"Here, let me get ahead of you," Moshe says, handing off the sleeping girl to her nanny. "I'll help you get around this boulder."

"It gets narrow here," she says taking his hand.

"We won't be able to get the carts through," he warns.

"Everyone unload the carts," the Master orders. "We'll have to carry our supplies. Take the carts and push them down this hillside."

The servants quickly comply. Lady Zhao grabs two water jugs.

"Let me help you, Mistress Zhao," Moshe offers.

"I'm okay. Moshe, stay with Ming and get us to our destination quickly. These jugs will keep me balanced. Go on."

Cook and the maids push the carts over the edge of the hill. The family watches as they roll down and disappear behind the trees.

"I am worried, Moshe," Lady Zhao sighs. "Will we become, like our belongings, a pile of shards and splinters?"

He turns to look at Ming. "A dear friend recently told me to put one foot in front of the other and not to look back."

"Yes, good advice. Let's go, Mama."

****

The family slowly hikes the narrow trail leading above the tree line. The moon disappears below the horizon. Soon the sun will rise and the family will be exposed. Ming leads the group along the ridgeway and down the backside of the slope. Around a large boulder, Suzhou Jian awaits. Nestled into the mountain walls, the bold sculptures welcome the Zhao family with glistening splendor. Even the dragon appears serene.

"Ming? What is this place?" Zhao Heng asks.

"We call it Suzhou Jian, Baba."

"We?"

"Jian and I."

Zhao Heng steps between the larger than life objects. He stops in front of the meticulously carved dragon, admiring the workmanship.

"Magnificent," he whispers aloud.

"Look over there, Baba, see the fisherman?"

Zhao Heng crouches down examining the carved figure—no prize at the end of the rod.

Ming recites: "The full moon churns the sea. The winds howl and cry—"

He finishes the poem, "Fisherman will go hungry tonight."

"Yes, Baba, and over there is your Lotus flower, and above you, your bird. And see up on the boulder? Your angry man is crouching on the rock, and you have met your dragon. These are your poems come to life."

The Great Poet is speechless. His heart stops beating for a moment and he is helpless to move. A sickness sits like a rock in his stomach. He rests his head against a Lotus petal. His eyes search Ming's face.

"Yes, Baba. The carver is Jian, my brother."

The name spoken aloud pierces his chest. Zhao Heng closes his eyes. Overwhelming sadness creeps into his heart, and he bows his head in shame. Tears well in his eyes as he folds his hands into his lap.

"Jian," he whispers, "my son."

Chapter Twenty-Six

In the pre-dawn hours, one lone carver sits in the dusty room etching feather patterns into a block of cherry wood. He sits hunched over, eyes pressed close to the surface. Jian is grateful that Mr. Guo entrusted him with the studio prior to leaving Shuzou. Here, in spite of the dust, he is able to breathe.

Soon after the siblings waltzed through the studio, the belt that rotated the old turntable snapped and turned to dust. The phonograph had played its last song. Jian hums to himself, recalling the melodies from the records he once played. He misses the scratchy sound of the needle dragging upon the vinyl and the hiss from the speakers. He dips a torn rag into a cup of oil and gently massages the figure emerging from the block of wood. Soon he is aware of someone calling his name.

A young soldier stands in the doorway of the carving room.

"Jian, the sergeant has ordered you to report at once," the soldier says.

"I see," Jian says without looking up.

The young man enters and moves closer, eyeing the carving. "Jian.

The orders were issued to arrest your father. Our unit marched to the House of Zhao."

"And did they find him?" Jian sighs without looking up.

"No, and they didn't find you there either, obviously."

Jian smiles to himself. "The family may have left to visit the aunties in Beijing."

"Jian," the young man interrupts, "you are under suspicion of warning your family and helping them escape. I am scared for you. We have been friends all our lives. Your father is my most revered teacher.

"If you leave now, I will tell the sergeant that I couldn't find you. You can go find your family. You can keep the Master safe. It is your father they want to punish, not you. Please, Jian, if you stay here, you will be branded a traitor!"

Jian squints at the shaft of sunlight in the doorway. He rises and turns to his friend. "You are my dearest friend, my comrade, my brother. I am grateful for your loyalty to my father and the House of Zhao. I will go—but, with you."

"No, my friend. Please, you need to consider what the Sergeant will do. You will be punished," the soldier pleads.

"I ask that before you escort me to the authorities, you give me a few minutes with my carving."

The soldier nods and retreats to the back of the room. Jian takes a small silk bag from his pocket and unwraps two tiny rubies. He stands back to admire his work—a figure of a large crane. The bird, fierce yet conflicted, sits perched, ready for flight. The neck is slightly crooked; the beak open in mid-call. One large wing fans out towards the sky, while the second wing is partially completed—encased inside the block of wood—unfinished. Jian glues the ruby stones into the eye sockets. He takes a step back and bows to the bird.

"I am ready to go with you," Jian announces.

The young soldier looks at Jian, at the mighty but tortured bird, and weeps.

"Please, my friend. I will be fine. I am the son of the Great Poet, Master Zhao. I will inherit paradise."

Chapter Twenty-Seven

Daybreak clothes the denizens of Suzhou Jian. Dewdrops kiss the faces of the children as they sleep. In a crevasse, Ming sleeps, lost in her dreams. Moshe rises to find Zhao Heng where he left him, kneeling on the ground next to the large Lotus blossom.

"Master Zhao," Moshe whispers, "how can I help you?"

The Master turns his head towards Moshe's voice. "I have spent the night in meditation. I have been searching for answers. How did this happen, and I didn't know?" he asks, gesturing at the sculptures nestled in the ravine.

"How did I not recognize the true virtue of my own son? Why did I work so hard to tamp down his spirit instead of celebrating the magnificence that is Jian? I have failed him. Look at this. I am but a small man sitting amongst this tremendous achievement."

Moshe places a hand on the shoulder of this broken man.

"Where is Jian now?" the Master asks.

"We don't know. Perhaps with the army," Moshe whispers.

The Master hangs his head and silently weeps.

"Master Zhao, I feel sure that he sent his friend to warn us. I believe he chose your safety above his."

Zhao Heng nods silently.

"I am grateful for your words, Moshe." He sits up straight, gathering some strength. "I've been thinking for a couple of days about your situation here in Suzhou. The Japanese are sheltering your people in Shanghai. You need to go and find your family. They must be very concerned about you, and you will be safer there than staying here with us. The NRA will not be as lenient."

"But, I must see that you get home safely," Moshe protests.

"Ah, but you have. We will be safe here in Suzhou Jian. When the Japanese have moved on from Suzhou, we will join you in Shanghai. Some of Lady Zhao's family is waiting for us there. Ming will guide you by the back road leading out of Suzhou."

Moshe helps the old man to his feet.

"If I have lost my son, I will forever find him here. Thank you for bringing me to Suzhou Jian. I will pray for your safe journey, that you will find your family, and that you leave in friendship. Go, my son. We will meet again."

****

They hike down the mountain in silence. Ming fought back her tears when her father woke her with the news of Moshe's immediate departure and insisted she guide him to the road leading to Shanghai. She hated knowing he would be going to another unfamiliar city. She had never traveled that far and only knew of the city as crowded and dirty. She worried that Moshe might get lost or ill. Why now, when life beyond Suzhou Jian is so unpredictable?

The pair reaches the spot where the trees rim the roadway. Ming slows her pace and stares at the horizon.

"It's going to take you several days," she sighs.

"I'm okay. Cook packed me enough food to last a week."

"Moshe, I'm worried about you going to Shanghai. It's crowded, and I hear it is dirty. Mama's family says people are getting sick."

"I know, but I need to find my family."

"We are your family, too."

Moshe sets down two jugs of water and his knapsack filled with food. His coat bunches from the little Torah secured around his waist. The chill makes his breath cloud the air, yet his skin stings with sweat. It is a heart-wrenching goodbye.

During the weeks he lived in Suzhou, he fell in love with the Zhao family, especially with one graceful, spirited girl. Although he feels overwhelming gratitude for her kindness, at this moment of leaving, he cannot find the words to express his love. He can only embrace, weep, and promise to meet again.

During the long walk out of the forest, Moshe felt numb. Now, the moment of leaving Ming tears at his gut.

"When you get to Shanghai, will you be searching for your school friend?"

"*Kenahora*—Elana will be waiting," he says.

"You love her?" She can feel his answer.

Moshe watches a tear fall from Ming's eye. He smiles sadly. "I will never forget our moment together in your garden, Ming."

"Never forget," she whispers. "Am I to be just a memory? You are so much more to me than that. Love is precious, right? Why is it wrong for us to have feelings for each other? Just because we come from different cultures? Why can't we find happiness together?"

"We did nothing wrong, Ming. Our feelings for each other are pure and hard to understand. It tears me up inside because my fondness for you is sincere. Believe me when I say that I wish we lived in a different world and that we had been raised under different circumstances. where you and I could make an acceptable couple. But, here in China and within my community, we must not cross that line.

"It isn't fair to you, or myself, and especially to Elana. I love her, Ming, and I need to find her. I need her in my life. Please try to understand. I have been surrounded by the most generous people, and still I have been alone."

She cries softly. "You are being so cruel, Moshe. My heart is breaking."

Moshe looks at her sadly. "I am so sorry, Ming. I do not want you to think of me that way. I came here under dire circumstances. My recovery took place in a foreign land, with a beautiful maiden who comforted and tempted me.

"My history is uniquely different from yours. Elana has been constant in my life. We are bonded with unbreakable understanding." He draws her close and exhales an anguished breath. "You are a treasure, Ming. Knowing you has been a special gift and I will honor you—forever."

She nods, yet finds no solace in his words. It feels incomprehensible that she would have to say goodbye to this young stranger who mysteriously arrived at her home, became her friend, and swept her off her feet.

He throws the knapsack over his shoulders and picks up the water jugs.

"Well," he says, awkwardly. His sadness is overwhelming.

"Do you think fate will ever lead me to the well like Rebekah?" she asks.

"Yes, Ming, I know it will and it will be you who offers water for the camels." She smiles through her tears. "Whenever you feel alone," he continues, "look to the nearest bird sitting up in a tree and know that the bird is never afraid of the branch breaking. Trust is not in the branch, Ming, but in its wings. You will find the love you deserve."

His lips brush her cheek. He tastes the salt from her tears. He secures the load he is carrying and takes his first step onto the road leading to Shanghai.

Part Five
Shanghai

Chapter Twenty-Eight

I am being punished—Elana sighs, curling her body into the alcove of the only window in the tiny one-room apartment she shares with her family.

The stench of urine and feces wafts up through the window from the street below. Stale air, hanging over the narrow alley, is so thick that it blocks out the light—*I am too stubborn to cry.*

The younger siblings need her to entertain them and the elders rely on her physical strength, yet the food has been meager and she has lost weight.

How many weeks have passed since their arrival in Shanghai, and then Hongkew, the City of Filth? She wasn't sure. There had been a long and cramped train ride and once they arrived in Vladivostok, all the Jewish passengers boarded a luxury ocean liner. Her father had purchased first class cabins. Each one included a personal Japanese valet who brought them food, played with the children, and attended to their needs.

The trip had been comfortable and Elana was grateful to be off the cramped train. This was the first time she had seen an ocean—vast like the Siberian ice fields. She felt her stomach flip and held onto the balustrades for support. Frosty air filled her lungs and her heart raced from the anticipation of her new life.

She desperately wanted to be able to share her adventure with Moshe, but with no way to reach him, she told herself that at least they were traveling under the same sky.

Kyoto, Japan, was supposed to be the final destination. On the train, travelers shared stories of the beautiful gardens, magnificent temples, and the warmth of the people of Japan. However, when the families stepped off the train in Vladivostok, they were told that the plans had changed. With too many refugees in Kyoto, the Japanese government was deporting all Jewish immigrants to Shanghai, China.

The unexpected news caused the families alarm. The Rabbi explained to his congregation that Shanghai was a major port city for the country of China. What he didn't know was that the Japanese had control of the port and that all the Jews were required to live in Hongkew, a crowded, stuffy ghetto filled with beggars and filth.

At the port of Shanghai, representatives from the Jewish Committee met the families. It was a welcome relief to be around people who spoke their language. The men of the Committee were anxious for Rabbi Lozinski to start a *yeshiva* for the religious Jews in Shanghai. The Japanese government had allowed the Committee to designate one building for worship. That is where they would cultivate the temple and the Rabbi would lead the congregation.

The walk from the port to the International Settlement yielded unimaginable sights. Chinese men sold fruit and vegetables from baskets that swung from poles resting upon their shoulders. Rickshaws dashed through the crowds, not pulled by horses but by humans! Elana and the families passed shops, cafes, and cabarets reminiscent of Vilna and Berlin.

A ball bounced off Akiva's leg and he returned it with a swift kick. He smiled, happy to see a team of boys playing soccer in an empty lot next to the Shanghai Jewish School.

The man from the Jewish Committee pointed out that the earlier refugees had built a self-sufficient community filled with hospitals, theaters,

172

shops, schools, and sports clubs. Elana and her mother noticed how the British, American, and European women were well- dressed, and yet for the Chinese, living conditions appeared dire.

"You can thank the *Sephardim,*" their guide said. "They brought their bank accounts when they arrived in Shanghai many years ago."

"But the Japanese didn't confiscate everything?" Rabbi Lozinski asked.

"No, they don't want to antagonize us," the man from the Committee replied.

"How is that?" asked Elana's father.

"They think we control the western governments. That *we* are the banks. That if they treat us well, *we* will finance their war effort."

"Then the joke's on them, yes?" the Rabbi mused looking down at his scuffed shoes.

"Indeed," the men agreed.

In spite of an uncertain future looming over the refugees, Elana was impressed by the fortitude of the human spirit. Judging from the booming life in the city of Shanghai, the early refugees had pulled off a miracle.

****

After the families' arrival, the Japanese order all Jewish refugees to move to an area outside the city known as Hongkew. The British and Americans are forced to live in another area of the International Settlement. In Hongkew, buildings are ancient and lack modern conveniences. It is a ghetto with invisible boundaries.

Although heavily patrolled by Japanese guards, Elana's mother is able to secure a pass to leave Hongkew and travel to the center of Shanghai. There, she purchases stockings, spices, razors and blades, makeup, and candy that she hides in pockets sewn inside the lining of her long skirt. Elana helps her mother run a small store out of their apartment. The extra income affords chicken for *Shabbat* dinner.

Rabbi Lozinski organizes a *yeshiva* in a two-story building at the end

173

of one of the narrow streets. There, he teaches the lessons on the Torah and *Talmud* to the religious men of the community. For the first time, he allows his younger children to attend the secular school nearby. The school provides one hot meal a day and the children enjoy the diversions of playing soccer and socializing with other young refugees.

In the evenings, the Rabbi sits with his children and reads them stories, practices their Hebrew with them, and encourages them to ask many questions.

Elana enjoys listening to these sessions but regrets that their hasty exodus from Vilna interrupted her own education. She has no time to spend learning. During the evenings, after helping her mother clean the dishes in a bucket of soapy water, Elana mends clothing. Most of the families trade their children's clothing, so many items collected are full of rips and holes. While she sews, her mind drifts faraway to the lush forest of her village. She listens to the Rabbi tell the story of Passover and pictures herself as Queen Esther, pleading with her husband to save her people.

Elana's mother nudges her back to the task at hand and at once the four stark walls close in, assaulting her senses with pungent odors. She ties a bandana around her face.

If the Nazis don't come to kill me, the foul air will.

She longs for the crisp ocean breeze as she wipes the sweat dripping down her forehead with the sleeve of her blouse.

If only I had my own private space, I'd sew in my underwear.

Everything in her family's one-room apartment is covered with a sticky film from the humidity.

Moshe's family shares the two-bedroom suite. It is crowded and at times the lack of privacy is humiliating. Every morning a Chinese woman appears at their door to collect the piss pots, dumping the contents into the street. Elana's mother constantly sprays the room with her perfume in a desperate effort to disguise the agony of their lives.

In an attempt to obtain some decorum, Elana's father rigged up a sheet as a divider in one corner of the room. It is sickening that the family is forced to cook and eat in the same room that serves as their toilet. Early in their arrival, the children became sick with dysentery. There is no escaping the heat and the odors of stale food and human waste.

Elana opens a window and, using a towel, fans the air into the room. She dusts the small table and sets out the dishes and silverware. The mismatched place-settings and chipped crystal goblets make a sad dinner table. Sergeant Ghoya, the Japanese chief of the Stateless Refugees Affairs Bureau—the self-proclaimed *"King of the Jews"*—will be a guest tonight at dinner.

Akiva called him *"The Slapping Man."* Every morning, the Jews who wish to leave the ghetto and go to work, attend school, or shop in Shanghai, line up in front of Mr. Ghoya's office at the police headquarters to obtain a daily exit pass.

Mr. Ghoya is a short man with a foul temper and a large ego. For reasons unknown, he possesses an aversion to people taller or thinner than he. Known for standing on his desk, he is in just the right position to slap his perceived offender in the face.

His brutality is infamous. If he didn't like a refugee's hair, nose, or clothing, if he demanded they speak to him in Japanese and they could not comply, he would send them to the typhoid infected prison where they would never return.

Mr. Ghoya is ugly, unpredictable, and has atrocious eating habits. Elana detests him. Her mother reminds her that making a friend with the enemy brings benefits. Mr. Ghoya's love for her cooking translates into passes for the covert shopping sprees out of the ghetto—no face slaps, or risks of incarceration.

The mothers perform miracles with only two hot plates; boiled chicken seasoned with saffron from India, rice with vegetables. While on her latest excursion Miriam purchased honey cakes and chocolate cookies from a Chinese bakery to serve her guest for dessert.

****

Mr. Ghoya announces his arrival with a pompous flair. He showers the children with candy and pumps the Rabbi's hand. Akiva cringes at the violin case tucked under Mr. Ghoya's arm. The children dread the

175

mandatory after-dinner concerts.

"Ah," Mr. Ghoya sniffs at the air. "I have brought you an empty belly, Rabbi."

"We welcome you to our home, Mr. Ghoya," the Rabbi says, offering him a seat at the table. "Please, sit and have some wine."

Elana helps her mother serve the meals. "Try to smile, Elana," Miriam whispers, "we need to stay on his good side."

"Does he have one?" Elana rolls her eyes at her mother.

"Hush, daughter," Miriam scolds.

Just as Elana expected, dining with Mr. Ghoya is as fun as eating worms. Mr. Ghoya pushes the meal around his plate. He separates the vegetables by categories; potatoes on the right, carrots and beans to the left. He arranges the chicken pieces, first lining them in straight rows, then rearranging the pieces to form circles around the potatoes.

The odd behavior is characteristic of the usual dinners with this unwanted guest. No one speaks, for fear of raising the ire of the bear at the table. Elana is shocked by the rudeness—*Did his mother not teach this wretched man not to play with his food at the table?*

Rabbi Lozinsky pours more wine and encourages Mr. Ghoya to drink. He scoops up a mouthful of food and grabs his glass, downing half of the wine in the process.

"Eh," he snarls, picking his teeth.

"You do not care for the wine?" the Rabbi asks, but Mr. Ghoya broods in his drink. "I sense, Mr. Ghoya," the Rabbi continues, "that the world is weighing heavily upon you tonight."

"Ah, my friend, I fear I am still bitter. The current events have my mind spinning."

"What troubles you?" Rabbi Lozinsky asks softly.

"The Nomonhan Incident bothers me!" he snarls again. "I don't appreciate being crushed by the Soviets when I warned my superiors in Tokyo that this was a disastrous idea in the first place."

"You warned them?" the Rabbi asks. The children sit silently.

"*Yes!* And history has proven me correct!" Mr. Goya slaps the table. "*Five—hundred—thousand*—troops slaughtered. *Thousands* of tanks and airplanes!"

Elana recoils as spit flies from the little man's mouth when he speaks. "Maybe now they will believe me!" Mr. Ghoya's voice rises.

"What was it they didn't believe?" the Rabbi asks.

"That our leader Masanolu—in Manchuria—had rocks in his head and stars in his eyes. Stupid, arrogant man!"

Elana hides her smile behind her napkin—*How the blind cannot see.*

"He was convinced he could take over Mongolia and march all the way to Stalin's front door in Moscow," Mr. Ghoya snickers. "I warned against attacking the Russians inside their own border! How could they underestimate the command of the Soviets? No, they just fell for the talk of Masanolu!"

"I see," the Rabbi nodded. "He didn't expect that Stalin would make the pact with Germany."

"*Exactly!*" Mr. Ghoya pounds on his plate and the children jump.

"Okay, I understand, but that is over now," the Rabbi assures him.

"Yes, yes, but now, we are switching tactics."

Elana is intrigued—*How stupid can this man be to speak of Japan's war strategies to the Rebbe, who is technically his enemy?*

"Really?" The Rabbi strikes a nonplused tone.

Mr. Ghoya downs the remains of his wine in one gulp and burps aloud at the table. The family is repulsed by his horrible lack of manners.

"No, no, we are giving up on the Soviets, although my idea was to stage a two-front war on Russia; Germany on one border and us bombing on the other. If they had listened to my plan and gotten Germany on board, we would be in an advantageous position. The Soviets would have nowhere to go and would have been forced to surrender.

"I should have commanded this plan. I could have ensured victory for Japan. Instead, we suffered a humiliating loss, we're going to focus on pushing southward, and I'm stuck here in this disgusting ghetto with a bunch of Jews!"

He fingers his cup of wine. Elana narrows her eyes. Miriam stares blankly at the wall behind her children. Rivka pushes her chair back and begins clearing the dinner dishes.

"I hope you saved room for dessert, Mr. Ghoya?" Rivka smiles but the little man ignores her.

"What is southward?" the Rabbi asks.

"Huh?" Mr. Ghoya takes another swig from his glass.

"Southward?"

"Oh, we are going to capture the United States of America. What a prize that will be for our allies and will help us save face. Annihilating the U.S. will prove to the Allies and enemy that Japan is the most powerful nation in the world."

"I wonder if the big fish you are going after will turn out to be a whale," the Rabbi muses.

"Ha," Elana laughs.

"Hush, Elana!" Miriam admonishes her daughter.

"Excuse me," Elana blushes, "I am excited for dessert. We have a special treat for you, Mr. Ghoya." She smiles at him sweetly and he reclines into his chair.

Miriam sighs and rises from the table. She fetches the dessert platter and presents it to the guest.

"Ah, wonderful. Chocolate and honey cakes. Yes, a rare treat!" he laughs. "You do well with those passes I give you, yes Mrs. Holtzman?" He winks.

"Yes, Mr. Ghoya. I am very grateful for your kindness," Miriam answers.

Elana looks at her mother with pity. Sometimes the humiliation is unbearable.

"And now we will play music," Mr. Ghoya commands. "Come children, get your instruments."

Elana's father pushes the rolled-up mattresses aside as the children assemble in an orderly circle. Mr. Ghoya raises his violin to his stubby chin and looks to Akiva.

"Give me an 'A,'" he commands.

Elana's youngest brother attaches the reed to his oboe and blows the note. Akiva readies his bow, and his sisters adjust their music stands.

"We will play Concerto in A minor. I assume you've been practicing since last time?" Mr. Ghoya asks.

"Yes, Mr. Ghoya," the children utter in unison.

"Good." He taps the count with his bow and the catastrophe begins. Mr. Ghoya is either tone deaf or senile, for his interpretation of the time signature would make Bach roll over in his grave.

178

Akiva struggles to follow the man who randomly plays certain bars too *allegro* and others too *adagio*. Mr. Ghoya closes his eyes, and with a grand gesture, sways while sustaining a chord on his violin.

"*Adagio!*" he calls to the children. "You must keep up with me."

Akiva looks to his father and rolls his eyes.

"*Forte!*" Mr. Ghoya commands.

Elana's little sister takes a deep gulp of air and blasts the mouthpiece of her flute. The sour note bursts through the little room with an ear piercing shriek. Mr. Ghoya puts down his violin and the room goes silent.

"This is a concerto, not an air raid, young lady."

Elana's sister rests her flute in her lap and lowers her head. "Excuse me, Mr. Ghoya," she sighs.

"Very well, you children need to practice more. We will try again next time, and I'm sure it will be just as Bach imagined." He hands them each a piece of candy from his pocket. "My respects to you, Mrs. Holtzman. A truly delicious meal."

"Thank you, Mr. Ghoya," Miriam answers, forcing a smile. "We look forward to your next visit."

Mr. Ghoya nods and collects his violin. He turns and slaps the Rabbi on the back.

"Wonderful evening, Rabbi." Then, poking Rabbi Lozinsky in the chest with his stubby finger he adds, "I don't know why the Nazis hate you people so much."

Chapter Twenty-Nine

"Twenty-one, twenty-two," Akiva sighs, patting down the layer of rice he laid along the windowsill. When the sun streaks across the ledge, the bugs crawl out to warm themselves in the warm light. Akiva flicks the bugs out the window and collects the grains of rice into a little tin cup.

"Is that your record?" Elana asks, pushing her needle into a wool skirt.

"Nope, last week I counted thirty bugs."

The bugs arc a long trajectory to the ground. Akiva follows their path as his eye catches a tiny dot at the end of their alley lane. He stands and leans his body out the window. The dot appears to be the outline of a man walking towards their house.

"Moshe," Akiva whispers.

"What's that?" Elana asks.

"It's Moshe!" Akiva yells.

"What? What are you saying, Akiva?" Elana runs to the window. The distance is too great. "No, Akiva, it can't be. You want it to be him but that's probably one of your Papa's students."

"Yes, yes, it's him! I can tell!" Akiva pulls away from the window and heads out of the room. He jumps to the bottom landing and runs out the front door.

"Moshe! Moshe!" Akiva shouts, racing down the alley.

Elana watches from the window, holding her breath—*Akiva must be mistaken. We haven't had a word of Moshe since we left Vilna. Poor Akiva.*

The figure steps into the lone stream of sunlight and Akiva leaps into his arms. Elana rips her apron off her body and catches sight of her reflection in a small mirror hanging on the wall—*Oh, not like this! I'm a mess!*

Her fingers snag in the knots of her hair. Elana runs to a box where her sisters stow their school supplies. She swipes her finger over a pad of dry pink paint and spreads the color on her cheeks and lips. Then, straightening her dress, she descends the stairs.

****

Akiva can't stop kissing the face of his beloved older brother.

"Whoa, Akiva," Moshe laughs. "You are going to push me over. Look at you. You've grown some in the months we've been separated."

"I can't believe you are here, Moshe. I prayed every day for you to come home."

"Well, today your prayers are answered. So, this is home now?"

"Where were you? How did you get here? Did you take the big ship like we did? I'm going to a new school. I'm playing soccer!"

Moshe laughs as Akiva's voice rings down the alleyway.

"How are Papa and Mama?" Moshe asks.

"Papa is at the *yeshiva* and Mama is shopping for food. We live up there, Moshe." Akiva points down the narrow lane to an apartment on the third floor. A figure of a young woman emerges from the doorway. Moshe's heart skips. Elana stands quietly and waits.

"I will go and let Papa know you are back," Akiva says, throwing his arms around Moshe's waist. "What is this under your shirt, Moshe?"

182

Moshe opens his coat and lifts his shirt, exposing the little Torah wrapped tightly around his waist.

"It's the Baby!" Akiva shrieks.

"Yes, Akiva. I brought the Baby for you!"

Akiva brings his *tzitzit* to his lips, kisses the fringe, and gently presses it to the Torah. He turns and runs down the alley. Like the day Mr. Bernstein gave him a mission, this time, his news will bring tears of joy.

Elana wants to run to the arms of her dearest love, but that would not be proper. Besides, one of her hands feels like it is cemented to the door jam and she can't let go. Moshe slows his stride, approaching her gently. He dreamt about this moment over a couple of months and now that it is here, it feels peculiar—lost, not found.

In their awkward silence they are thinking more about themselves than of each other. Elana worries that the long months of traveling has left her gaunt and unattractive. Moshe wears the dirt of the road and the confusion in his heart for Ming. Is it possible that time apart has caused a rift in their feelings for each other?

He looks at her face, she lifts her eyes; their hearts warm. A tear glistens on her cheek and the pink powder runs down her face. Her features are more defined now, her dress—rumpled, yet she is the most beautiful sight.

He reaches out and takes her hand—she takes a breath, folds her hand around his, and leads him up the stairs to their home.

Chapter Thirty

What does it mean to have everything and nothing at the same time? Stateless, no identity, a wandering alien on foreign soil, and yet with Elana, Moshe has found his home. This is to be the holiest day of his life. He will stand before God and his congregation and pledge to clothe, shelter, and protect the woman he has loved since he was a small boy. He smiles and accepts the good wishes from the elders and students who toast the union with songs of praise.

In another room, Elana sits on a chair—the queen for the day—enjoying the excitement bestowed upon her by her family and guests. Rivka and Miriam break a plate to remind the couple that as a broken plate cannot be easily repaired, so too a broken relationship cannot be easily mended. Moshe watches Akiva and his youngest brother dance in celebration.

If only Levi were here to see him dressed in his white *kittel*, then everything would be perfect. It has been a few months since any letters arrived from America, and Moshe's heart sinks, wondering if his brother might be unaware of his wedding. Levi would be amused that after so

185

many years, Moshe's love for Elana never faltered.

Even the time it took to ride a train across the desolate Siberian landscape, the months spent in the emerald gardens of the house of Zhao, and every laborious footfall down the roadway to Shanghai, was calculated as a mile closer to his beloved. All these events have led him to today—a spiritual union folded into a time when futures are impossibly unstable.

In a matter of an hour, Moshe will become a husband and Elana, his bride. Two singular spirits will join to become one soul.

Standing in the doorway of the synagogue, flanked on both sides by her parents, Elana pauses. Moshe draws down her veil to cover her face, symbolizing the bride's purity and reminding people that it is the character of the bride that counts, not the physical appearance. Even so, the young, smart woman standing before him takes his breath away. With her thick curls framing her high cheekbones, strong nose, and full lips, she is a vision wrapped in aged satin and lace. The gown, once worn by her mother, is a cherished memento of a happier life.

In preparation for the marriage, the two have been fasting. A gurgle emanates from Moshe's stomach, and he can feel the blood rise in his face. Elana's eyes laugh through the mesh of her veil.

Under the *chuppah*, Rabbi Lozinsky officiates the marriage of his second born son to the daughter of his closest friends. It is a good match, a proper match, and there is a comfort level between the two that will provide the bond they will need to face life's challenges.

Through her veil, Elana catches Moshe's eye. Her skin glows from the thick stale air that fills the sanctuary. She takes her first steps towards the marriage by circling her groom seven times; thus, building the walls of their new life together.

Rabbi Lozinsky recites the marriage blessing and offers the couple the first glass of wine, signifying life. The couple take turns sipping from the glass. Moshe's hands quiver as he places a gold ring on Elana's right index finger. He looks into her eyes and recites—"Behold, you are consecrated to me with this ring according to the Law of Moses and Israel."

Rabbi Lozinsky holds up the *ketubah*, the marriage contract. Hand painted leafy vines rim the borders that frame the words. Written in

Aramaic, the ancient language of the Jewish people, the document declares that Moshe will provide Elana with food, clothing, a home, and be attentive to her emotional needs. Two members of the family sign the *ketubah*, then witness Moshe adding his name at the bottom. The Rabbi presents Elana with her marriage contract.

For the second part of the service, Rabbi Lozinsky, along with several honored guests, recites the seven blessings. Moshe tries to conceal an itch from under his robe and Elana fidgets under the weight of the veil—*Is his father, the Rebbe, purposely slowing down the chanting of the prayers?*

His stomach growls. Elana giggles. The Congregation utters the final—"Amen."

The second sip of wine is the sweetest. Rabbi Lozinsky wraps the glass in a cloth napkin and places it on the ground next to Moshe's foot.

"Although this is a happy day, we remember in sadness the destruction of the temple in Jerusalem," he announces to the congregation.

Moshe closes his eyes—*This is really happening.*

The pounding of his heart drowns out the sound of the glass shattering beneath his foot. Elana claps and the congregation yells—*"Mazel Tov!"*

He opens his eyes. It is done. He is joined in marriage to the love of his life.

****

The strains of a scratchy violin waft through the air into the *Heder Yichud*, the private room where Moshe and Elana can break their fast. Elana pulls off her veil and laughs. "Can you believe Mr. Ghoya is a guest at our wedding?"

"Sounds like he's the entertainment too," Moshe laughs, then cringes at a sour note from a distant violin.

"Mama made me invite him. She said, 'Get in bed with him or spend your nights sleeping on a prison cot.' I hate that man. Pfft!" She spits on the floor.

"Elana, today you are the queen, my queen, and that is all that counts.

You know Levi wrote in his letters that in America, the couples kiss each other under the *chuppah*."

"In front of everyone?"

"Yes."

"Oh, I couldn't, Moshe," she blushes.

"Yes, but could you now? It's just us." He smiles shyly and steps towards her, reaching his arm around the small of her back. She closes her eyes as he leans in. Her full lips brush against his. He draws in her breath, tasting the remnants of the pastry she snuck before the ceremony. He touches her face; skin moist, hair slightly damp.

This kiss is not Ming's kiss. It does not ignite the spark that jumped through his body, sending waves swirling through his head and spinning thoughts at a dizzying pace—mysterious and dangerous. Instead, this kiss, Elana's kiss, brings warmth, comfort, safety—a kiss that lingers on the lips long after they part. Moshe's finger becomes tangled in a curl of Elana's hair.

"Ooh, sorry," he laughs, untangling the knot. "It doesn't want to let go."

"It never will," she answers slyly, helping free his hand from her tangled mass. He knows her so well, and yet now that they are joined in marriage, she feels new. There is so much more of Elana to discover. He hopes a lifetime will pass, and still he won't solve the mystery that is his beautiful wife. Serenity pours over the couple.

This is where I'm supposed to be.

"Is it okay for me to feel this happy?" she whispers. He folds Elana's body into his and they hold each other in silence. Her tears drip down her cheeks, spotting his sleeve.

****

Rabbi Lozinsky opens the party to everyone residing in Hongkew. Elana and Moshe have never seen such a feast. Every guest who owns a hot plate brought a dish. The Jewish Committee donated dishes, cups, and silverware. As an exception, Mr. Ghoya allowed a Chinese bakery to deliver a cake. He toasts the couple with his personal bottle of wine, which he made clear was not to be shared.

Into the evening, the men dance together on one side of the *mechitzah,* while on the other side, the women ply Elana with marriage advice.

Mr. Ghoya conducts the band, wielding his bow like a saber. The musicians are fearful that if they don't perform in "Ghoya Time," they will all be slapped or imprisoned.

For the moment, Moshe can relax. His family surrounds him, joined by many people he knew growing up in his village of Vilna. Eyes normally filled with the pain of the daily hardships are softened by his joy. He is aware of laughter, not just from the children, but also from the adults. People look at him with a new sense of pride.

Elana walks over to her side of the room where a long satin ribbon separates the party.

"Moshe," she calls.

Moshe joins her. "Yes, my love?"

"I wish I could put this day into a snow globe like the one that Levi sent you. Remember?"

"I do, except Levi wrote and told me he thought the gift was funny because it doesn't snow on the Golden Gate Bridge."

"It doesn't? What a strange souvenir."

"Levi said the globes are for the tourists."

"I think that is very unfair of San Francisco to mislead people!"

"Ha, you are funny, Elana. One day when we visit, you can pack all our snow and bring it with you to share."

"Thank you for marrying me, Moshe," she blushes.

Under the ribbon that separates the two, he secretly squeezes her hand. She smiles and turns to join the women.

On this wedding afternoon, soft pinks and bright oranges wash the sky in iridescent hues while below, in the alleyways, swatches of indigo extend across the roads and buildings, casting harsh lines and shadows.

In the distance, two Japanese soldiers detain an elderly man who is demanding to join the wedding party. The old man appears distressed, insistent on being allowed to pass. One of the soldiers marches up to Mr. Ghoya, who sets down his baton.

"Rabbi, your attention!" Mr. Ghoya demands.

The Rabbi joins the little man, flanked by his soldiers.

"There is a Chinese man demanding to speak with your son, Moshe. I will not permit him to interrupt this wedding and will have my soldiers remove him at once."

"Mr. Ghoya, I appreciate your consideration of my son and his bride. With your permission I will speak with this gentleman. But please—our guests—there is no party without your music. Tonight, we celebrate this *mitzvah*. Please, play."

"Yes, of course! Gentlemen! Instruments!" Mr. Ghoya commands.

The Rabbi summons his son. Moshe squints into the darkness where several people huddle beyond the Japanese guards. An instant recognition surges through his head.

"Master Zhao! Papa, it's Master Zhao!" he yells, running towards the group.

The guard swings his rifle at Moshe. Rabbi Lozinsky jogs towards the soldiers.

"It's okay, my son is familiar with these people. Please lower your rifle, this is a wedding."

"Master Zhao! What a blessing that you have arrived on this day!" Moshe exclaims.

"Moshe, I fear our appearance is poor timing." The Master bows his head.

"Master Zhao, may I present my father, Rabbi Lozinsky."

"It is an honor, Rabbi," Zhao Heng bows.

"The honor is mine, Master Zhao. I am grateful for the kindness you showed my son."

"Please, may I present my wife, Lady Zhao Shu, and my daughter, Ming Hua." Moshe turns to see Ming step out from the shadows.

"How wonderful to see you, Ming. You look well. Is Jian with you?" Master Zhao shakes his head. A tear rolls down Lady Zhao's face.

"Moshe?" The voice calls from behind. The group turns to see Elana standing a short distance away.

"Elana, please, come and meet my friends. This is Master and Lady Zhao." Moshe says. The Master and Lady bow.

"Very pleased to meet you. Moshe has told me many stories about your family with great fondness," Elana replies.

She turns her attention to the shy girl standing to the side, eyes turned towards the ground. Ming's wooden foot peeks out from underneath her robe.

"Ming, this is Elana, my bride," Moshe says with pride.

Ming looks up at the couple. The bride radiates warmth. Ming manages a smile, but Elana senses a heart broken. For many days after his arrival in Shanghai, Elana plied Moshe with questions about his journey from their home. Ming was a name that came up often in the stories he would share.

Elana understood how fear creates extraordinary circumstances and she could imagine how unbearable loneliness could force a person to seek comfort from a stranger. Moshe's relationship with this sweet, shy girl meant something more than a casual acquaintance. Still today, Moshe pledged his love to *her* in marriage. If Moshe felt a sincere fondness for Ming, it would be because she gave him kindheartedness, therefore, Elana would embrace her too.

"Master Zhao," Elana says, "would you and your family do us the honor of joining our party?" Turning to Ming, she offers her hand. "Please say, yes. You shall be as a sister to me."

****

Rabbi Lozinsky asks for quiet, Mr. Ghoya lowers his baton, and the band stops playing.

"We are grateful for this day," the Rabbi begins, "not only for the marriage of our wonderful son, Moshe, to his beloved Elana, but for the welcomed surprise of the Zhao family here tonight. Master Zhao and his family clothed, sheltered, and cared for Moshe during a challenging time, and we are blessed that we will have the opportunity to reciprocate with our friendship."

Master Zhao bows. "Thank you, Rabbi, and to your gracious family. If I may say a few words ...."

191

"Yes, of course, please," Rabbi Lozinsky says, ignoring the looks of annoyance from Mr. Ghoya.

"Rabbi, you have raised a remarkable son. Moshe is a dedicated worker and possesses great virtue. I'm sure you are as proud as we were inspired by him."

The Master reaches into his satchel and slides out a package wrapped in purple Chinese silk and tied with an ivory satin ribbon. He hands the package to Moshe and continues, "Moshe, after you left us, a student of mine arrived at Suzhou Jian and said that we were free to leave for Shanghai. We were told that Jian reported to his unit and offered to be my proxy. He was taken to a prison outside of the city and arrested in my place for the crimes of subversion to the cause."

Master Zhao turns his face and steels himself after a moment. "Please excuse me. This is a very difficult thing for me to understand. Rabbi, I am sure you know well the deep love parents have for their children, and you understand how that love will surpass any difficult issues between you. I am very proud of my son."

"I believe Jian went to prison with the strength of knowing, that in doing so, his family is safe," Moshe offers. "I hope you will find peace with his decision."

"Apparently Jian's action impressed his commander, so instead of staying in prison, Jian was sent to a work farm in the north. My student warned that if I was caught in Suzhou, I would be detained and sent to a work camp."

"And your poetry writing?" Moshe asks.

"It seems I will have to suspend my writing for a while unless I'm willing to exalt the virtues of the Communist Party."

The Master and Moshe share a smile.

"But," the Master continues, "that is not why I am here. Upon leaving Suzhou, Ming insisted we stop at Mr. Guo's studio. She wanted me to see where Jian disappeared to all these years, to smell the trails of the fragrant resins and see the place through Jian's eyes. Ming took us into the carving room in the back, where I became breathless standing in the presence of Jian's latest creation; a large crane, fraught with despair, its wing fixed within a block of wood—grounded."

"I can only imagine how powerful that carving must be," Moshe

192

sighed.

"Yes, indeed," Zhao Heng agreed. "As we were looking around the room, Ming noticed a package addressed to you."

"To me?"

"Yes, and included was a note to me asking that I deliver this to you in Shanghai upon our arrival. I am satisfied that I am fulfilling Jian's request today."

Moshe accepts the package. He unwraps the paper, the ribbon slides away, and the silk fabric covering the item drapes upon the floor.

"Oh, Jian," whispers Moshe, cradling two wooden Torah shafts to his chest. He holds them up to the guests. On the top of one, sits an intricate carving of a dragon. His mouth spews a fiery breath while its tail coils tightly around the shaft. Sculpted onto the second shaft, a lion rears, regal—proud. Both appear fiercely protective of their charge.

"Look, Akiva!" Moshe says to his younger brother, "my dear friend, Master Zhao Jian, carved these beautiful *atzei chayim*."

"For the Baby!" Akiva claps.

"Yes! For the Baby!" He turns to Master Zhao. "I am overjoyed and filled with admiration for Jian's thoughtful gift. We will cherish his beautifully carved *atzei chayim* and I will attach them to our little Torah. Months ago, he honored me by writing a letter in our little Torah. I'm proud to know that the Torah also embodies the spirit of my cherished friend."

Zhao Heng bows. Moshe watches Ming and Lady Zhao, surrounded by the women. He catches Ming's eye and smiles.

"Come, Mr. Ghoya," Rabbi Lozinsky commands. "Please play some music. We must celebrate this day."

The band strikes the opening to a traditional folk song. Moshe and Elana are seated in chairs, then hoisted into the air.

A guest hands the fallen Chinese silk fabric to Moshe, who in turn hands one end to his bride. The couple is paraded around the hall joined by a flurry of people, dancing, singing, and laughing.

For one evening there are no Japanese soldiers, no threats of imprisonment, no putrid narrow alleys, no crowded homes, no hunger, no loss, and no war.

Chapter Thirty-One

Piles of books lie waiting, gathering dust. They, like the people who turned their pages, have traveled great distances and weathered the trials of wear and tear. Moshe loves them all. He treats each one that arrives in his small shop with reverence.

As there are no Torahs to repair, Moshe puts his skills to use as a book-binder, patching worn leather bindings, gluing torn pages, and restoring books to their former glory. In the process of his work, Moshe has become the local librarian, catering to a community thirsty for mental stimulation and escape.

For a year he has enjoyed getting to know his customers and keying into their particular interests. A recommendation from Moshe meant several hours of welcomed relief from the choking air and relentless hunger.

In spite of the daily struggles, Moshe is grateful for the small joys. Marriage to Elana has been a blessing. Their first night together after their wedding ceremony had been awkward. The anticipation of holding her naked body against his was so powerful that when the moment finally arrived, they were too overwhelmed to consummate their union.

Instead, they found peace lying on their small mattress, bodies pressed together, holding each other tightly. Elana pleaded repeatedly for Moshe not to let go. He, in turn, kept promising that he'd never lose her again.

The first week was spent mostly staring at each other in disbelief. Moshe loved watching Elana glide around the small, sparsely furnished room that they now called their home. It is impossible to feel completely safe when the threat of dying is lurking behind every corner. *Home* is a temporary concept.

"Does it sadden you, my love?" Moshe remembers asking her one night while she was making a small pot of potatoes and vegetables on their hot plate.

"What's that, Moshe?" she asked, not turning around.

"That I'm not able to provide you with a proper home?" His voice settled into his chest. Soon another couple would be moving into this dank, crowded room. There would be no privacy, no time to enjoy building a life together; just eating, sleeping, and keeping their head down.

"It isn't a tent in the desert," she laughed. "Look at me, Moshe. We are fine. Okay? We are fine. Now eat."

That was Elana, always providing comfort with her words.

As the weeks passed, their nighttime hugging turned into exploring. Nothing in his countless hours of studies with the most learned Rabbis, or his whispered discussions with the *yeshiva* boys, has prepared him for the wonderment and joy of body embraced with body.

Moshe wonders why his studies focused on intimacy being practiced for the obligation of procreation and not enjoyment. The human touch is a comfort and intercourse, an irrevocable bond. He feels a profound sense of responsibility to Elana, who entrusts her body to his care. When his fingers brush the surface of her breasts, she purrs. The mysterious place between her legs is moist and welcoming.

Once they are joined, he inside her, he soars beyond the physical pleasure to a faraway spiritual realm. There, he lingers for a moment until his ecstasy abates and he floats down onto the mattress on the floor of their tiny room. Wrapped within her embrace he knows that Elana is right—they are fine.

****

The bell on the door of the shop signals the arrival of a young mother with her four-year-old son. Moshe enjoys children's visits. He can't wait for the day when he will be able to read aloud to his own children.

"Good afternoon, Mrs. Meyer. What can I do for you today?"

"What might you have that would interest little Haim?" she asks, pushing the boy ahead. "He has become very restless, a handful."

"Well, let me look. I'm sure I can find him something interesting." Moshe moves a stack of books that take up part of the floorspace. "Would you like to sail boats in the South Pacific? Or, trek with the penguins in Antarctica? Maybe ride a stagecoach across the plains of America?"

Haim's eyes widen watching Moshe select a few books off a shelf.

"Maybe a safari in Africa would be fun. Or, how about—"

An air raid siren blast ricochets off the stone buildings and brick walls. Mrs. Meyer grabs hold of her son.

"It's okay, perhaps it will be cancelled like the ones before," Moshe assures her.

"Yes, of course," Mrs. Meyer nods, releasing her hold on the boy. "Well, what do you think, Haim? Where would you like to go?"

At an altitude unseen, one hundred B29s fly over the clouds blanketing the Shanghai sky. Within seconds, the piercing wail of the sirens mixes with the roar of oncoming danger. Inside the small bookshop, the windows start to vibrate and the piles of books slide down from their shelves, fanning onto the floor.

Mrs. Meyer scoops up her son and runs out into the street. A shrill sound cuts through the thick air. There is no mistaking the whistle that heralds the bombs as they plunge towards the ground.

Moshe grips the bookcase attached to an inside wall and crouches to the floor. Books fall down around him. The explosion rips through the shops nearby, tearing apart walls and shredding glass. Plaster falls from the ceiling. Moshe stumbles over his books and staggers into the street where people are running, screaming.

197

The sky rains with fire. Silhouettes vaporize in the smoky haze. In the street, Moshe makes out the figure of young Haim frozen with fear.

Where is his mother?

Another whistle roars overhead. Moshe scoops the boy up into his arms and jumps into a sewage trench alongside the roadway.

The bomb slams into the two-story building nearby. The building crumbles to the ground. Concrete and masonry dissolve into a fine powder spewing over the street, burying Moshe and Haim under a thick mound of debris.

It takes only a few seconds for the American bombers to destroy and level many buildings in the Hongkew district of Shanghai. Though the mechanical roar of a hundred bombers announced the arrival of impending doom, their sudden retreat leaves a shroud of silence.

****

The dust settles, revealing the devastation. Once the mecca of the ghetto area, teeming with refugees, the street is quieted. Death lies in mid-pose on the ground, pooling blood onto the roadway. Mountains of rubble remain where residences and local businesses, less than a minute ago, lined the narrow alleys. In the distance an ambulance siren wails.

A soft breeze settles dust upon the bodies. A young child staggers amid the devastation, crying out for her mother. An elderly man drags his beloved wife down the street until he collapses over her body.

Moshe heaves his body from under the mound of crushed cement. The mixture of dirt and concrete dust plug his nostrils. He gags, coughs, and spits. He blows his nose on his sleeve and bats away the ash circling his face.

Haim!

The force of the blast had separated his hold on the boy. Desperately, he claws at the mound, pulling out pieces of metal, pushing aside the powder and ash. Reaching deep into the dirt he finds a tiny arm and pulls Haim to his feet. The boy vomits up dust and throws his arms into the air.

"Again! Again!" he laughs with wide-eyed glee.

Twenty feet away, Mrs. Meyer lies in the dirt, bleeding. A sliver of shrapnel protrudes from her thigh.

Moshe lifts the boy and steps over bodies to reach the woman. He sets Haim down next to his mother and flags down the ambulance.

"Your Haim is okay," Moshe tells the frightened woman. "Go with these men. They will take you to the hospital." Turning to the boy, he says, "The doctors will help your mama."

The little boy nods. Mrs. Meyer reaches up and grabs Moshe's arm.

"All over in a second," she whispers.

"Yes," Moshe agrees, surveying the devastation that was once his bookshop—"just one second."

****

Across the ghetto the buildings escaped the onslaught and sustained lighter damage. Moshe races up the narrow staircase and into his tiny apartment. The dining table had been pushed up against the inside wall away from the window. The bedspread drapes down all three sides and is topped by the mattress.

Moshe smiles and leans down. He parts the quilt curtain to find Elana huddling in the far corner, her arms wrapped tightly around the little Torah.

"Are you practicing building a children's fort?" he smiles.

"I guess since you are here and speaking to me that it is safe to come out?" she whispers.

"Yes, my love, give me your hand," he offers, but she won't release her grip. His heart warms at the sight. "I can't even find the words to tell you how much I love you, Elana."

"Well good, Moshe, but find the words to help me move. I'm scared, and I'm paralyzed."

"We are okay. We are blessed. You are fine. Hand me the Torah and I'll help you out."

"What happened, Moshe? I don't understand. All of a sudden, I heard the sirens, people were running down the alley, yelling to find shelter. I didn't have enough time, so I just started throwing things on top of the table and praying."

"You did the right thing. I don't know exactly what happened. Some people were saying it was the Americans. I don't know why they would bomb Shanghai. We need to find Papa and our families and make sure they are all right."

"Was it bad where you were, Moshe?"

"Most of the shops are ruined. Mine has a lot of damage."

"Oh, Moshe, I'm so sorry."

"All I could think about was you, here alone," he says sadly.

"I'm sure you are worried about your books. Are they okay?" she asks surveying the room. "Oh, the window is broken."

Moshe tugs at a piece of metal wedged into the floor. He looks at Elana and suddenly the harsh reality sets in.

"*B'ruch Hashem* that you are safe, Elana," he utters, his voice cracking.

Elana takes the piece of shrapnel from his hands and places it on a bookshelf.

"I admit I was terrified, but I knew you would come for me. Tonight, we will celebrate our good fortune that we are alive and unhurt."

Moshe looks at the shrapnel on the shelf. "Now we have a Shanghai souvenir."

"I would rather have bought a snow globe," Elana says.

Moshe smiles at her ability to find sunlight in the storm. He settles into his chair and watches her resume her cooking. How has he been so lucky? Why were they spared? He is not any more special than the others who lie dead on the hot pavement. He rests his head in his hands.

Elana kneels at his side, placing her head in his lap. His fingers tangle in her hair and for the first time since the exile from Vilna, he cries.

Chapter Thirty-Two
Hongkew, 1945

A restricted living environment doesn't only pertain to where one sleeps at night, what food is offered, where to work, go to school, or play. It also the affects the control of news available, especially information about the war.

Censorship is so pervasive that people meet, huddling in dark shadows, spreading rumors and innuendos. Moshe hears it all from his desk in his damaged bookstore. His customers are starving for news of the well-being of their families and friends and the conditions of their homes and cities so far away.

Yet the local newspaper, the *Shanghai Jewish Chronicle,* paints a life in the ghetto filled with normalcy—announcements of babies born, engagements, the opening of a stage production of *Pygmalion,* offers at the butcher's, advertisements for the hair salon, a clothing store having a sale, watch repair available at the jewelry store.

It is as if Shanghai is its own little world and Hongkew, its one-mile state filled to capacity with stateless people. So, it came as a surprise when a customer mentioned that the Japanese were going to allow a radio broadcast that evening from the President of the United States. Moshe tries not to get excited because there have been too many false moments. When the Germans surrendered there had been great rejoicing. The refugees spoke of going home, of picking up their lives prior to "the interruption."

The Japanese squelched any notion of peace; they were still at war with the world. Their business wasn't finished. Restrictions, already difficult, became unbearable. For Moshe, censorship came to his store in the form of Japanese soldiers who confiscated many volumes of books that had been brought to Shanghai by the refugees. Perhaps the news from the President of the United States of America will bring hope.

****

"It is an Atomic Bomb. It is the harnessing of the basic power of the universe. The force with which the sun draws its power has been loosened against those who brought war to the Far East."

The voice of American President Harry S. Truman crackles through the speakers of the radio in Rabbi Lozinsky's apartment. Moshe and Elana's families, along with a few refugees, gather to hear the latest development in the war between America and Japan. President Truman is speaking words whose meanings are incomprehensible:

"More powerful than 20,000 tons of TNT."

"Complete devastation."

"A milestone achievement that will aid the U.S. and her Allies in defeating the tyranny of the Japanese."

The words make Moshe shiver. None of the people in Shanghai can imagine devastation worse than the day the American bombs rained from the sky, killing 31 refugees and over 100 Chinese. Now, the American President is warning the world of the total annihilation of a nation, and with it the obliteration of innocent lives.

Japan made the decision to join Hitler as an enemy of Western Europe and the U.S. They committed atrocities too horrible to comprehend, but throughout his years in China, Moshe had witnessed the struggles of all the innocents: Japanese, Chinese, and European refugees. Many, both ally and enemy, never wanted their lives disrupted by the corrupt people who bullied their way into power.

Master Zhao was right, Moshe thought—*The innocents are the ones led to the slaughter.*

Listening to the President's speech gives rise to an anger churning deep inside—*Why weren't we able to speak out? Where were our voices? Why are we rolling over? Where is our strength? We are an intelligent community. We have produced some of the greatest thinkers and achievers in so many areas: medicine, science, art, and literature. Did we allow this to happen? When the war is over, will we learn from this experience and be able to prevent it in the future? How many died today in Hiroshima? And the Americans are planning on dropping another? Will Japan heed this warning, or will their greed cloud their humanity and allow their culture to become extinct?*

Akiva runs over to a map of the world hanging on the wall and tacks a pin over the city of Hiroshima. He has been marking all of the Allies' advancements and defeats since arriving in Hongkew. The number of pins has been growing.

"I don't know, Akiva," Moshe sighs, "after tomorrow there might not be a Japan to tack your pin onto."

****

Paper leaflets drop from the sky declaring the Japanese surrender. The invisible fortress that confined the refugees vanishes—alleys and avenues, vacant of soldiers.

The Japanese are preoccupied and fail to notice where the refugees travel, nor do they care. They lost their campaign to dominate the world and now have to return to their homeland in disgrace.

In their absence, Moshe and thousands in his community are left to discover truths so unimaginable that minds fail to comprehend the enormity of it all.

Words flow from lips and into ears—*Nazi death camps, burned alive, gas chambers, starvation, and horrific medical experiments.*

Each day, stories flow out of Eastern Europe, seeping into the ears of Shanghai.

In the afternoon, Moshe and Elana walk to the office of the Committee for Assistance, to check the paper lists pinned to the front wall of the building: "Survivor Lists." So many names—missing.

Moshe hasn't found his mother's sister, his uncles, his cousins. Many of Elana's family haven't made the list. Missing are the names of neighbors, shopkeepers, people who supported his life in Vilna.

Where are the Bernsteins? He should be sorting their mail. And Mr. Penkowski should be offering fish hugs to everyone who stops by his stall. Their names should be on the list. They should!

For weeks the refugees wander around Hongkew in a catatonic state of shock. Food tastes bland to the tongue, conversations dwindle down to half-hearted nods, children stop playing soccer games. Grief turns to anger—tears shed form pools of sorrow.

Rabbi Lozinsky inherits the daunting task of counseling the bereft. His words do not bring comfort. For the first time in his life as a Rabbinic teacher and leader, he feels like a failure. He cannot fathom the atrocities. He plays the scenarios in his head. The children—slaughtered. The elders—shot. Bodies piled two stories high behind a storage shed. Dogs tearing the flesh of the escapees. The once able-bodied, forced to work and then starved. Medical experimentation on *live* subjects.

The Rabbi is asked over and over a question he dreads—*Why?*

Why were we exterminated? *Why* didn't anyone help?

And the question most heartbreaking—*Why did God abandon us?*

Moshe joins his father to sit and pray. They are paralyzed with grief.

****

One evening, Mr. Ghoya appears in the doorway of Rabbi Lozinsky's tiny apartment. He looks around and draws in the aroma of chicken stewing in the oversized pot on the small portable stove. For the first time, the short, mean man does not command the room. He appears sunken and sallow. He refuses the Rabbi's invitation to join the family for a meal.

"It's over," he admits in a quiet voice.

"Yes, *Baruch Hashem,*" the Rabbi nods.

"I'm leaving. I've been called back to Tokyo, or what is left of it."

"Ah, I see," the Rabbi nods.

"Before I leave, I want to say something to you. I want you to know that though we were enemies in war, in another place and time, I would have considered you a friend. During our years in Shanghai, I have become very fond of you and your family. I will miss our evenings of conversation, your wife's dinners, and your children's music."

Akiva and his sisters stifle their laughs. They keep their eyes on the little man in the doorway. The Rabbi stays in his chair for a moment, then slowly rises, joining Mr Ghoya in the doorway.

"Well, Mr. Ghoya, I am glad to hear your sentiments, and I hope you will go back to your homeland with a new appreciation for the Jewish people."

"Yes, yes, of course," mutters Mr. Ghoya.

Rabbi Lozinsky studies the man. He knows Mr. Ghoya's convictions and patriotism for his country run deep in his veins. He knows the man is a liar and untrustworthy.

Still, it doesn't hurt to plant a few seeds, forge a new path. "You know, you and I share something in common. We are built to desire a better world for our children and ourselves, no?"

"True," Mr. Ghoya agrees.

"Yes. Well, if you value our friendship then I will request of you a favor."

"Of course, Rabbi."

"Good. Go home, make a family. Teach the young ones how precious is this gift of life. Tell them how evil and selfish greed for power destroys the fragile balance of the world. Show them by example, by *your* example, how it looks to uphold a life filled with respect and compassion. Give them a life without hate."

Mr. Ghoya rocks back on his heels as the Rabbi continues. "This I know will be a challenge for you, but not an unattainable goal," the Rabbi muses. "Go home and let me hear that you are working in that direction, then I will be able to find peace in my knowing you."

Mr. Ghoya looks up at the tall man. For the first time he has lost the urge to slap a Jew. Instead, he allows himself this moment. He knows that he is truly in the presence of a great man, a man who never faltered under the harshest conditions. He bows and backs out of the doorway.

When he is out of the building, the children clap and break out their instruments, finally free to play. The Rabbi joins Moshe at the window.

Mr. Ghoya appears in the street below. He turns, looks up, and nods.

"Thank you, Papa, for speaking our truth," Moshe whispers.

"I pray that we are never robbed of our freedom again, but that wretched little creature, as irritating as it was to placate his foolishness, is of flesh and blood. I had to feed him, but I didn't have to like him."

Moshe smiles and places his arm around the elder man's shoulders. "I am thankful today, Papa."

"Yes, Moshe," agrees the Rabbi. "The irony here is that in spite of erroneous ideas about the Jews' worth, the Japanese saved us. We were lucky the Chinese didn't have visa restrictions, though with the Japanese occupying their country they didn't have much of a choice." The Rabbi sighs.

They watch the cruel little man slink down the narrow alleyway and vanish into the shadows.

Chapter Thirty-Three

The ravages of war empowered the heart and brought connections in ways Moshe never imagined. Love came to him in several forms—Elana, his cherished wife who he adores, Ming, the desired temptress who awakened deep physical longings, and Master Zhao—mentor, with whom he bonded over the love of the written word and who introduced him to the art of poetry. Invigorating. Frustrating. Astonishing.

Poetry writing becomes a newfound obsession. Moshe finds the process intriguing; organizing words into stanzas, brief sentences filled with metaphors and innuendo, balanced with synchronicity and rhythm. With Master Zhao's encouragement, Moshe finds his voice, turning his thoughts outward, capsulizing moments of his life spent at his home in Vilna, the fear of leaving, the dirt and sweat of his escape, the gut-wrenching loss of loved ones at the hands of the German soldiers, the new friendships, anger, and hope.

Each poem produces a peaceful sensation that washes over his body. He lives for that feeling—that calm—though its duration is brief. *The*

Shanghai Jewish Chronicle publishes some of his poetry. The Rabbi finds the poetry odd, and yet he is proud of his son and doesn't discourage him. Elana is just proud, enjoying the attention from the other wives.

Inside his bombed-out bookshop, boxes are stacked and marked with shipping labels containing an address to Oakland, California, U.S.A. Most of the bookshelves are empty, the broken front window is boarded, and the stale air chokes with dust.

"So, you are packed," a soft voice whispers through the misty haze.

Moshe startles and looks up from his papers. He squints at the figure of a girl silhouetted in the doorway.

"Ming! Come in. Please. I'm so happy to see you!"

He clears a box and motions for her to sit. In spite of the wooden foot, she avoids the obstacles with grace. She is his fragile doll, his warrior, his muse. Quietly, she sits and examines the mailing label on the box.

"Baba said you are leaving tomorrow."

"That is true."

"Would it be too forward of me to say I wish you would not go?"

"Oh Ming, of course not. To you, I owe my life. You are the reason I will leave Shanghai with a heavy heart. You will always be family to me."

She raises her eyes. "Family, yes, but nothing more, Moshe?" She rests her hand over her heart.

"Yes," his breath catches in his throat. "Ming, I have cried and smiled thinking of you. I admit that the feelings I have for you run very deep. At times I have questioned the doctrines of my religious life and why we can't be more than friends.

"Perhaps these traditions are wrong. Maybe years from now marrying out of our faith and race will be acceptable. Maybe I am just not brave enough to go against my practices and long-established traditions.

"I have struggled with my conflict of loving you, of longing for you, touching your hair, your face. I prayed, what if I followed my carnal desires? Will God understand if I abandoned my dear Elana, my bride?

"In the end, I needed to bow to the stronger desire. I honestly would not feel comfortable losing my family. I would be shunned by my community and never allowed to see my family again. To them, I would be dead, and they would mourn for me. That bond, my faith, and community run deep in my veins.

"If I stayed with you, dear Ming, I would ride on a wave of euphoria until the tide ebbs and then my resentment would flow in. I would hate you and hate myself, and that would be too deep a hardship."

Ming focuses on the small circle she has drawn in the dust. "We would first be in here," she explains, placing two dots into the center of the circle. "Yet, your heart would be here." She draws a heart on the outside.

Moshe looks at her sadly. "I pray that you can understand that what I'm telling you is coming from a sincere place. I honestly would be heartbroken to lose Elana. I treasure you both. I am only telling *you* how I feel.

"I am not supposed to be conflicted, but I am. Perhaps this is a lesson to show me that no person owns the attributes of everything he or she desires. It is instead the acceptance of what is missing and the cherishing of the unexpected that makes for a special relationship."

"Your words make sense, and I am saddened that we have to part. If I can't live with you as my love, I will die not having you as my friend."

"Nonsense!" He kneels at her side. "Ming, our lives will change, but there are no boundaries or time in friendship."

"Oh, Moshe, I miss you already."

"And, I you. Listen, something else. Your father has told me he is very concerned about living in China once the Communists take over. They will strip him of his money, home, and possessions. I am hearing talk about a possible civil war. He worries about Lady Zhao and you and your little brothers and sisters. As soon as we are settled in San Francisco, I will send for you and your family. We will all make a life in a new world. Together."

Ming's tears drip onto Moshe's shirtsleeve. "And I pray," he continues, "that Jian will be freed and join us in America."

Ming runs the fine, silky fringe of the *tzitzit* through her fingers. "You are the first man I fell in love with," she smiles.

Her words sting. He stands and retrieves an envelope from his desk. "I wrote something from me, to you."

She slips the envelope into her robe pocket. Moshe looks out the front door to the empty street outside. What he is about to do is against the rules of propriety, however, ever since his arrival in Shanghai, Elana has embraced Ming whether in stories or in person. She never questioned Moshe's time in Suzhou. Elana innately recognized the importance of the friendship between her husband and Ming. In turn, she welcomed Ming into her heart. That respect and deep understanding is part of what makes Elana so cherished.

Though breaking a law of touching a woman other than a wife would be unforgivable, Moshe cannot predict when they will be able to speak again, so he folds Ming into his arms, holding her in a tight embrace.

"Please tell your parents that I will send them money for your travel expenses and the required documentation."

She nods as they pull apart, and tears well in her eyes. "Well ...."

"Ming," saying her name breaks his heart, "this is only just another day."

Chapter Thirty-Four

The "SS Marine Lynx" is a fairly new Navy transport vessel—523 feet long and 72 feet wide. It accomodates 3,845 troops. For this mission, she is sailing 3,000 refugees to freedom. Built to house Navy seamen, each passenger has a narrow bunk to sleep upon and is responsible for keeping his personal areas clean and tidy. The quarters are cramped, with men in steerage and women housed on the deck above. Only women with young children sleep in cabins.

Early in the voyage, many passengers spent hours leaning over the railings. The choppy seas were very disagreeable. After a week sailing the open ocean, the passengers got their sea legs and were able to enjoy the food and activities the sailors provided. For many people, the trip marks their first time tasting an orange or a banana. In the evenings, the sailors amuse the passengers by screening movies and producing talent shows.

"How Levi would laugh knowing the great Rabbi of Vilna is watching Hollywood starlets parade on the screen in strapless gowns! For once Papa is happy that Levi established a life in America." Moshe notes the irony.

As soon as the war was over, Levi sent all the documents needed for the family to travel. He signed letters proving sponsorship, provided living arrangements, and secured jobs for Moshe and Akiva. The Rabbi will have a position at a synagogue in Oakland, where Levi lives. For Moshe, the ship's cruising speed, at 17 knots, is not nearly fast enough.

****

Strains of Bach reach the ears of the passengers on the forward deck. They are met with melancholy and anticipation. Moshe's younger siblings play the pieces that remind the refugees of their homes. Moshe hands Elana an orange he has peeled. She breaks off a slice and hands one to Akiva.

"Thanks, Moshe, but I'm not hungry," Akiva says.

Moshe looks sadly at his younger brother. Lack of sleep and appetite have been common complaints amongst the refugees. He attempts to cheer up his family by covering his teeth with the orange peel and flashing a wide smile. His younger siblings stop playing and run off screaming. The war has sucked the joy out of life.

"Oh Moshe, you scared them," Elana scolds.

"Sorry, I saw one of the sailors doing this and it looked funny." He tosses the orange peels overboard.

"You must promise me that we will grow our own orange tree when we get a yard."

"Of course, anything you want," he answers. Ever since they received news of horrors of the concentration camps, it is difficult to believe in a future.

"It's going to be okay, right?" she asks hesitantly.

"Yes, my love."

"But, it's another foreign country."

"Yes, but we will adapt."

"I feel kind of nervous," she sighs and fans herself.

Moshe straightens up. "Well, you shouldn't be. The American women need you to show them how to open ketchup bottles!"

"What? Oh, that stupid advertisement that Levi sent you. You remember that?" She laughs, then recovers.

"How could I forget? The saying made your hair stand up straight, and that was a miracle." He smiles at the memory.

"Yeah, humph. 'So easy a woman can open it!'" she shouts to the open sea. "Well, Mr. Advertising Man, you'd better have your ketchup bottles lined up and ready when I step on your land!" For a brief moment, they share the memory.

****

A small pine box slaps against the steel hull inside the steerage cabin. Only a few inches of metal casing and wood separate the little Torah from a vast, cold ocean.

Moshe opens the case.

How are you faring, little one?

The little Torah sleeps comfortably nestled in a bed of plush white satin.

Moshe had hoped that after Jian's release from the work camp, his friend would have been able to build a small wooden ark for the journey across the Pacific Ocean. However, Jian's focus was consumed in nurturing the growth of the People's Communist Party movement—there was no time for favors.

Moshe worries about his friend. He wonders if Jian comprehends the implications of the Party's "message."

Will there be internal fighting between the Nationalists and the Communists for control now that China is embattled and economically drained? Will Jian truly enjoy his life under the rule of Mao Zedong?

Master Zhao expressed many doubts about the character of Mr. Zedong.

Moshe feels badly for the Master—*There is so much fear and sadness watching your son adopt ideas which demand a lifestyle so different from your own. Will Jian be forced to forsake his family?*

Moshe's request to build a wooden case was an imposition. Still, Jian took the time to visit the man who built coffins for the poor people living in Suzhou, and a couple of months later, Master Zhou delivered the case.

Moshe rolls up a shirt and secures the case against the hull to stop the knocking. Lying upon his bunk, he is aware of every ache in his body—every itch tickling his skin. Thinking about the loss of his family and friends who stayed behind quickens his gut. Since the end of the war, sleep has eluded him. *Why were we spared? When we reach our new home, how will I prove myself worthy of having survived?* Even Elana has confided feelings of rapid heartbeats and night sweats.

The pitch of the large craft heaving its hull against the rolling sea lulls him into a meditative state. He thinks about his true love struggling to sleep in her berth on the deck above. His arm dangles at his side; his hand rests upon the cold steel floor. He misses the warmth of his love sleeping beside him. He takes a deep breath and releases the air slowly.

It is comforting to know she is near, not like the lonely nights spent on the Trans-Siberian Railroad car gazing out the windows at the endless vast emptiness of the ice fields. He'd wondered if he would ever see her again, or where he would send his letters. He remembers when he arrived in Shanghai, delivering them to her in person.

For days they huddled together and shared their travels. He delighted at her resiliency and marveled at her competency. He felt proud of her and she, in turn, worshiped him. Most of all, he appreciated her heart. He exhales one long slow breath; they are going to be fine. They are the lucky ones. They have each other, their families, and they will start a new life. This is what he tells himself. If he could only enjoy the peace.

****

"I have never felt a breeze so soft," Elana says, dangling her fingers over the railing. Moshe watches Diamond Head loom in the distance. After almost two weeks of watching tilted horizons, the "SS Marine Lynx" pulls into the Port of Honolulu, Hawaii, to refuel and restock supplies. The passengers are allowed to leave the ship and visit the city for a few hours.

At the bottom of the gangplank, Hawaiian women welcome the travelers with fragrant leis. A young boy approaches with a tray of sliced pineapple. Moshe and Elana taste the exotic fruit. The sweet juice runs through their hands and drips down their arms.

"Everyone is so friendly here," Moshe says, licking the sticky juice from his lips.

"I learned they call it the Aloha spirit," she adds.

"Hmmm. Aloha spirit. Are they always like this?" he grunts.

"Not sure, Moshe, but with weather like this and constant ocean views, I would be able to be friendly all the time." Her words mask her truth as she pounds on her chest to slow her heartbeat.

Moshe slips his hand into Elana's as they stroll along the beach.

"Have you ever seen such a beautiful place, Moshe?" She tucks her bare feet into the sand.

"I wish I could share your enthusiasm, but I'm sort of feeling ill," he replies.

"What's wrong? Your stomach?"

"No, my mind. I feel conflicted. Am I supposed to be happy now?"

"I can't even speak about it," she says with sadness.

"I ask myself—was there something more we could have done? Why are we walking on this white sand while others perished? Did God spare you and me for a reason?"

"Do you think the American people will see us survivors as cowards or heroes?"

"You saw the newspaper photos, Elana. The people, *our* people, forced to walk into the ovens, pits full of naked bodies. Those are the heroes. Not me. I know Papa says we now have to pick up and go on, but I mean, how can it be that a short while ago we managed to live through inexplicable evil and now we are walking on a pristine beach with flowers around our necks, eating a sweet fruit and nodding at smiling people?"

A shiver runs through his body.

"It's just wrong, Elana, all of it. I shouldn't be here. I feel guilty. I'm losing my faith."

Elana takes his arm. "Come, Moshe. Let's say a prayer." She guides him to the water's edge. The sea laps around their ankles. Elana removes her *lei* and kneels down into the water. "Please, Moshe, I need to hear the *Kaddish*."

Moshe plants his feet into the wet sand and looks out at the sea. His voice quakes reciting the prayer for the dead—"*Yitgadal veyitkadash shemei raba, bealma divera chireutei veyamlich malchutei, bechayeichon uveyomeichon uvechayei dechol beith Yisrael, baagala uvizeman kariv, veimru: amein.*"

The wind whips the palm trees and battles the current; the water swirls into counterclockwise circles. At once, a powerful force grabs Moshe by the throat. His head spins. Air blows across his vocal chords; he is wracked with rage and remorse. *"Yehei shemei raba mevarach lealam ulealmei almaya!"* he yells.

The ocean, with a powerful fury, kicks up the waves. Pushing. Beckoning. Teasing. Destroying. The tide rises, swirling the foam around their feet, gripping hard.
Moshe's arms fling into the air.
"Yitbarach veyishta bach, veyitpaar veyitromam veyit-nasei, veyithadar veyitaleh veyithalal shemei dekudesha, berich hu, leeila min kol birechata veshirata, tushbechata venechemata, daamiran bealma, veimeru: amein."

He weeps—one tear for every cherished lost soul. *"Yehei she-lama raba min shemaya vechayim aleinu veal kol Yisrael, vei-meru: amein."*

A wave splashes Elana, grabbing her *lei* from her hands and tossing it into the whirling vortex of the angry sea.

Moshe's throat is raw, and he can only whisper, *"Oshe shalom bimeromav, hu ya-ashe shalom aleinu veal kol Yisrael, veimeru: amein."*

Elana sits quietly, numb, until the roar of the waves drowns the sorrow of their broken hearts.

Chapter Thirty-Five

"Moshe, Moshe wake up!" Akiva's voice calls from a distance. "Moshe, come on, wake up!"

Moshe feels a warm breath against his ear. He opens his eyes, but the steerage cabin is pitch black.

"What is it, Akiva?" he says, recognizing his younger brother. "Are you ill?"

"No, Moshe, get up. There is something you have to see!"

Moshe wipes his face with his coat and follows Akiva to the viewing deck outside. One by one, passengers awake and walk out onto the decks. The sun, still low on the horizon, illuminates the fog stretching over the water.

"There, look!" Akiva points into the distance. "What is that? A spire?"

The ship cuts its speed to ten knots as the Golden Gate Bridge rises above the ocean.

"Oh, Akiva, it's the top of the Golden Gate Bridge. Isn't it magnificent?" Moshe exclaims with a sudden burst of energy.

"I never imagined it so big," Akiva whispers.

"Breathtaking, to be sure. And to think, men built this bridge."

"I can't believe it."

Moshe places his arm around Akiva's shoulder. The refugees stand together in awe, with only the sounds of the gulls crying and the hum of the ship's engines to compete with the roar of the sea. The fog parts and the bright orange structure looms into view.

A lone violin plays a lilting melody, bittersweet and haunting. The refugees huddle together and the tears fall. The sailors drop their chores and join the crowd on the deck. It is a tradition that whenever their ship returns home to the San Francisco Bay, they link arms and sing *"God Bless America."*

Moshe finds Elana and his family. They hold each other tightly, listening to sounds of the San Francisco harbor welcoming them home.

****

Once docked, and the big ship engines shut down, the passengers are herded into cavernous buildings that serve as processing and detention centers. Fortunately for Moshe and his family, the wait is only a few hours. Interrogation officials bring the family into a smaller room for their interviews.

The officer is stern, but the interpreter is friendly. Moshe presents their documents and settles onto a metal chair facing the officer who reviews each line and scrutinizes each person.

"Your papers are in order, but who will vouch for your sponsorship?" the officer asks.

Moshe looks over at the interpreter, who shrugs. Suddenly the door opens and a winded young man bursts into the room.

"Hello! Hello! This is my family! I'm here. I'm here."

"And you are?" the officer asks.

"Levi Lozinsky," he says presenting his identification. "The eldest son of Rabbi Lozinsky. I am the family's sponsor."

Moshe stares at his brother in disbelief. His appearance is so ... American—khaki pants, striped button-down shirt under a vest, his hair held in place with some kind of pomade, and in his hand he holds a Panama hat. Moshe's mother bursts into tears and reaches for her son. He turns and nods at his father.

"Shalom Alechem, Papa."

The Rabbi smiles, his voice is frail. The long struggle has worn down his spirit.

"Alechem Shalom, my son."

****

"Levi, this is yours?" Akiva screams, dancing around the four-door 1942 Ford parked at the curb.

"Furniture must be a good business," the Rabbi says.

"Yes, Papa, I am doing well."

The family is so enamored by the bright burgundy vehicle that they fail to notice the young, attractive, blonde woman standing to the side. Levi takes her arm. "Mama, Papa, may I present, Nancy."

"I know you!" Akiva shouts. "You are the lady in the photo that Levi sent to Papa. Right Levi? Papa got very angry."

"Akiva!" Rivka's face blushes.

The young lady stands awkwardly in front of Levi's family. "Hello," she utters shyly. "It's a pleasure to meet you."

Elana looks to Rivka, unsure how to respond. They study the floral dress with the cinched-in waist on the pretty blonde.

"How very strange," Rivka whispers in Yiddish.

****

The time to settle into the three-bedroom unit in the Fillmore District of the city, that Levi secured for his family, was brief. Word had spread throughout the community that the renowned, learned Rabbi Lozinski and his family had arrived from Shanghai. Stories about the son Moshe, a young *sofer,* were particularly intriguing.

Clergy, representing various synagogues and churches, congregants, local politicians, wealthy patrons, and *yeshiva* students, fill the grand sanctuary with eager anticipation. Rabbi Lozinsky walks down the aisle of the grand hall on the arm of his eldest son. Moshe follows close behind carrying the wooden box that secures the precious *Sefer Torah.*

The congregation stands in respect as the family makes their way to the *bema* in the center of the sanctuary. The Rabbi motions for the congregation to be seated, then leans towards the microphone.

"Good afternoon and thank you for this warm welcome to our new home. This morning you have completed reading the last *parsha* of the *Sefer Torah.* An entire year has passed since we began reading and studying the Torah which represents our lives.

"Many of you have discussed and argued the laws and contemplated the lessons of moralities and decencies. This is a wonderful achievement. You must all give yourselves a pat on the back. Today we bring to you a special gift of a *Sefer Torah,* which my son Moshe wrote with his own hand. While it usually takes a year to complete, he had a little interruption," the Rabbi says with a twinkle in his eye. "I am proud of his accomplishment, and now he will be able to resume his work."

The hall is shrouded in wonderment, for perched regally on the top of the Torah's shafts, the magnificently carved lion and dragon shine in their new surroundings—resolute, strong, proud. Moshe slips off the velvet cover and opens the scroll.

"One day I will share with you my story, but not today. This is *Simchat Torah.* It has been a long road for my family, the Jewish people, this little Torah, and me, so today I am going to break the bondages of suffering and oppression by calling for *simcha*—joy.

"I invite you to join me in thinking about what joy means to you. Sure, you know intellectually that joy means pleasure and bliss. Frankly I— and I'm sure most of you—are not experiencing blissful thoughts at this moment in our lives. That is exactly the perfect scenario to tell yourself, 'I will have joy,' that we are the lucky ones. We are here together in this beautiful synagogue, in this exciting city, in this welcoming country. Be touched by the emotions that live in your hearts, feel the spiritual bliss that celebrates within your souls. Then, both universally and personally, you will be at peace."

What does *relief* sound like? Perhaps for some it can be found in a quiet sigh or the rush of a breath escaping the lungs. For Moshe, relief is felt in the soul of the familiar melodies reverberating throughout the hall and climaxing in triumphant jubilation. It is the strength of having survived that upholds his beliefs.

The little Shanghai Torah is the testament for whatever doubts he might have felt when the bleakest days left him lost and abandoned; all is righted in the words of this text. Words he, a young *sofer,* etched with ink and quill into the parchment.

He holds the little Torah against his chest, breathing life into the scroll. Magically, the expressions on the carved dragon and lion, once fearful and scary, appear wistful and serene.

"Welcome home," Moshe whispers and with one smooth motion, hoists his cherished treasure high into the air ....

Part Six
Los Angeles, California
The Present

Chapter Thirty-Six

... for the congregation to see. Brandon knows that his friends, sitting restless in the audience, are only attending his *bar mitzvah* for the promised party, DJ, and chocolate fountain. For him, this day brings a mixture of emotions. Performing is not his thing. His stomach flips as he thinks about the speech he will be giving.

The Rabbi told him to picture the thing he loves the most and speak to that. For Brandon, that "thing" is the sea. His mother calls him her "water baby." He shares his appreciation with his grandfather, who taught him the love of sailing. Mostly, he never feels more alive than the moment he paddles his surfboard out beyond the breakers and drops into a curling wave.

The cantor's tenor voice resonates off the walls of the newly built synagogue. The building's modern architecture is in stark contrast with the splendor of the ancient scrolls that line the simple pinewood ark. Brandon sits in a chair on the *bema* and watches the Rabbi from behind. He is familiar with the story that ties the little Torah to his temple; how a young Eastern European man had saved it from fiery destruction and carried it some 5,000 miles—from Vilna to Shanghai—wrapped around his waist.

Though Brandon is fascinated with the tale, it doesn't seem possible. He does, however, have a curious connection with the little Shanghai Torah. Something about the words, the melodies, the chanting, transports him to a place of tranquility and away from the teenage angst churning through his body.

Sometimes while practicing his Torah portion, he would imagine the letters leaving the parchment, swirling around him, chanting with audible voices.

During his year of preparation, he couldn't wait to dive into the many lessons and debate the Rabbi. He would purposely study the arguments that are written along the borders of the pages of the Talmud and then shower the Rabbi with many hypothetical scenarios. He presented so many philosophical and intellectual interpretations that the Rabbi was challenged to do research, and thus he was dubbed '*The Little Scholar.*'

During study sessions, when the Rabbi wasn't looking, he would gently trace his fingers upon the letters. Each character appeared to be thicker in the center, then taper off, forming defined and beveled edges. He wondered about the young *sofer* who had held the quill dipped in the ink—*What was he thinking about when he drew little crowns at the top of the letters or flipped one edge like a tail?*

The writings spoke to him, and occasionally, frustrated him. He relished the passages and the study, yet was eager to find answers which at times seemed unattainable. The importance of the Shanghai Torah presented a mystery that had sent him on an unexpected journey and helped him find a purpose within his community.

****

Nervousness cramps his stomach. When he was studying and practicing, he felt confident, but on this day, he feels uneasy.

Will he be able to chant all the blessings correctly? What if his voice cracks on a high note?

He wipes his damp hands along his prayer shawl. He shifts in his chair as the Rabbi calls him to the *bema.*

"Yamod, Baruch ben Mordechai v'Shosana," the Rabbi chants.

Brandon rises and joins his parents next to the ark. He stares at the carved shafts that crown the little Torah; the dragon hisses, the lion growls, and his knees weaken.

"Brandon," the Rabbi continues, "when we Rabbis spend our days teaching Torah we hope to inspire people to feel what we feel. How can we engage the students so that they not only learn with their heads, but also experience the joy with their hearts?

"When you read from the Torah, you bring the wisdom of our tradition into your heart. You feel the blood of Abraham, Isaac, and Jacob run through your veins. You find the wisdom of Moses and the strength of Joshua, and when you feel that, and when it lives in you, then you know what it is, not just to be a Jew, but also to carry the burden, the privilege, and honor of Torah into one's life.

"So, when we pass this Torah from one generation to the next, we give you the gift that will guide you on your own path."

The Rabbi hands the little Torah through the family generations—first the grandparents, who pass it to the parents—and finally it nestles quietly in Brandon's arms. He looks out at the congregation as they begin to sing.

The speech. The sweat drips from his hands, running down the sleeves of his brand-new jacket. He wonders, will he bore his friends?

The Rabbi calls the names of his parents for the *Aliyah,* the blessing before the reading of the Torah. Brandon watches his father kiss the fringe of his *tallit,* then touch the scroll. His mother and father say the blessing together, and then the Rabbi reads a passage. Afterwards, his parents recite one more blessing and move to the side.

It is now his moment. He looks out at his friends, who stare back intently. The Rabbi opens the Torah to Genesis, the first story, chronicling the time of new beginnings. Brandon looks at the Hebrew letters and hesitates.

The words turn to lines and shapes, floating above the parchment.

Heat radiates beneath Brandon's new suit. A cough disrupts the silence. The anticipation of this moment is overwhelming. He opens his mouth; his voice emits a whisper.

The Rabbi looks kindly at the boy, then points to the first word in the passage.

"Black Fire," he whispers, then slides his finger up to the empty spaces between the letters and continues, "on White Fire."

Brandon doesn't understand—*what a strange thing to say?*

He shifts his weight from one foot to the other. The Rabbi's finger hovers above the parchment. Brandon leans in closer towards the parchment.

What is Rabbi trying to tell me?

"The letters, the Black Fire," the Rabbi continues, "and in the spaces? The White Fire ...."

Brandon looks back down at the parchment. The letters settle down onto the parchment, in perfect alignment, like obedient soldiers. He follows the direction of the Rabbi's finger and at once, he sees it. The spaces between the letters—the White Fire—contains a secret that had been hidden imbedded within the layers of parchment for so many years.

Stains.

Stains of sweat, exuded through the pores of the skin, the body's reaction to heat, physical exertion, illness, and fear. Not just any skin, Moshe's skin, mixing with the residue from Brandon's finger. DNA left behind from a young man who risked his life to save one precious treasure. Brandon jerks away and looks at the Rabbi, who smiles and nods.

"The story was real," Brandon whispers and begins to understand.

Stains—the evidence left behind by a young scholar to teach the lessons of responsibility and courage. *Stains*—the unconditional love uniting one person from the past to one in the present. *Stains*—knowledge once gained, destined to be passed on. *Stains.*

Yuanfen—fate or destiny that brings people together: Moshe to Master Zhao, Moshe to Elana, to Ming and to Jian, relationships formed that are meant to endure a lifetime together. The binding force is a small handwritten Torah that traveled around the world.

*Yuanfen—Moshe to Brandon—*together, the Black Fire—the physical, the old soul present in a teenage body. The White Fire—vast and uncertain, full of possibilities and choices, defining Brandon's future. The infinite space where his spirit is allowed to grow, learn, and comprehend.

Brandon steps back and looks out at his friends, his grandparents, and his parents. Moshe's sacrifice and legacy flow through the blood of this young boy. He picks up his silver *yad,* places it underneath the first word and, finding his voice, he reads aloud—

"Bereshit."

✱✱✱✱✱✱✱✱✱✱✱✱✱✱✱✱✱

A Poem for Ming

How will you know me?

How will you know me?

When emerald leaves fade beneath the brushing frost.
When waterfowl skim the rivers to chase the sun.
And blossoms bring forth, a new season.

How will you know me?

When fawn-like beauty becomes no longer vibrant.
When lives apart grow distant with each second
passed.
And faces pass by, unfamiliar.

How will you know me?

When your touch on my lips has left your fingers.
When memories once vivid cannot be recalled.
And eyes once luminous, have yellowed.

How will you know me?

Listen, for it will herald its arrival in the breeze.
An unmistakable presence will surround you.
And, instantly, you will know me.

You will know me in the sound of my voice.

Epilogue

Today, the little Shanghai Torah, rests peacefully in an ark located at Stephen S. Wise Temple in Bel Air, California. In an interview I conducted years ago for the temple magazine, founding Rabbi, Isaiah Zeldin, recalled how the Torah came to the mountaintop.

"We wanted a little Torah to use for teaching our children. In the mid-sixties, the bookstores on Fairfax Avenue carried Torahs on consignment. We put out the word, and Mr. Solomon, of Solomon's Book Store on Fairfax, called us. He said that a man who had arrived in the States from Shanghai needed money and wanted to sell a small Torah. Temple member Ben Winters generously purchased the Torah for us."

In 1969, a former student of Rabbi Zeldin's started a small temple on Merced Island, Washington. Since this temple didn't have a Torah, Rabbi Zeldin and the congregation offered the little Torah on loan. Rabbi Jacob Singer, from B'nai Torah Temple, was thrilled that now his students would be able to study for their *b'nai mitzvahs*. He vowed to be personally responsible and he would guard the little Torah with his life.

Little did he know how prophetic that promise turned out to be.

On June 9, 1977, arsonists set fire to Temple B'nai Torah's newly built synagogue. Against the advice of the fire department, Rabbi Singer grabbed a fireman's vest and hat and raced into the burning building. He saved two Torahs.

Shortly after the fire, the little *Shanghai Torah* returned to Stephen S. Wise, now at its present location off Mulholland Drive. Rabbi Zeldin recalls with amusement the note he received from Rabbi Singer: "Thanks for the loan, but I've had enough of the responsibility."

Cantor Nathan Lam is now the guardian of the *Shanghai Torah*. "It's very old and small so it's hard to read. But it's a great symbol of our lasting heritage." Cantor Lam also notes that the small size makes the Torah easy to transport. "We brought the little Torah with us to Spain for my nephew Alex's *bar mitzvah*. We got permission to use the Synagogue of Rambam, in Cordova, where a service hadn't been held since 1492, when the Jews were expelled from Spain."

The Torah also traveled with Cantor Lam to Poland and Budapest. It even took an unscheduled trip when the airline misplaced it. Fortunately, it was located and returned. "And, I'm not done with it," he continues, "I plan to take it to Israel soon, and one day, I would like to bring it on a trip to Shanghai. Then it will make a full circle."

Cantor Lam had a new mantle made, giving honor and respect to the *Shanghai Torah*.

Glossary

Adonai – Hebrew for G–d.

Atzei Chayim – Hebrew for the shafts or mantels holding the parchment of the Torah.

Baba – Chinese for father.

Baruch Hashem – Hebrew for "Blessed be the Name" (or Blessed be G–d).

Bema – the podium where the Torah is unfurled for reading.

Bereshit – Hebrew for 'in beginning.'

Boychick – slang for a boy; youngster; kid.

Bubbe – Yiddish for grandmother.

Challah – a loaf of rich white bread leavened with yeast and containing eggs, often braided before baking, prepared especially for the Jewish Sabbath.

Chuppah – a wedding canopy used in Jewish weddings.

Dal – the letter "D" in Hebrew.

Dovaning – the act of rocking and swaying while praying.

Heder Yichud – a private room where the bride and groom spend time after the wedding ceremony. Symbolizing consummation.

Kashrut – the set of Jewish religious dietary laws.

Katubah – a handwritten marriage contract, often with decorations.

Kenahora – a Yiddish saying for warding off evil spirits.

Kiddush – the blessing said over the wine.

Kittel – a white robe worn in the synagogue on major festivals and weddings.

Kosher – allowed to be eaten or used according to the dietary or ceremonial laws.

Kugel – a baked pudding or casserole, most commonly made from egg noodles or potato.

Mantel – a cloth Torah cover made of satin or velvet and decorated with embroidery or fringe.

Meshuge – Yiddish for crazy.

Mechitzah – a divider separating the men and women's sections of the synagogue.

Mezuzah – a case attached to the doorposts of houses, containing a scroll with passages of scripture written on it.

Mitzvah – Hebrew for "commandment." Can also mean a good deed.

Nu – Yiddish for general word that calls for a reply. It can mean, "So?" "Huh?" "Well?" "What's up?" or "Hello?"

Nun – Hebrew letter "n."

Parsha – a weekly Torah portion.

Passer Montanus – a Eurasian tree sparrow.

Payot – the side curls on a man's head.

Rebbe – Hebrew for a great spiritual leader and teacher. Also known as Rabbi.

Sampan – a flat-bottomed Chinese wooden boat. Some include a small shelter on board.

Shabbat – Holy day of prayer and rest beginning sundown on Friday and ending sundown on Saturday.

Sabbath – another word for Shabbat.

Schweinebraten – a German roast pork dish.

Sephardim – The decedents of Jews who left Spain and Portugal after the 1492 expulsion.

Shafts – the wooden doweling that the Torah scroll is attached to.

Shiksa – a disparaging Yiddish term for a non-Jewish woman.

Shomer Shabbos – a person who observes the commandments.

Shtetl – the small villages where Jews lived in Eastern Europe.

Simchat Torah – marks the completion of the annual Torah reading cycle and is one of the most joyous holidays on the Jewish calendar.

Sofer – a Torah scribe.

Shul – Yiddish for Synagogue.

Tallit katan – a prayer shawl.

Tref – Yiddish word for any form of non-kosher food.

Torah – Jewish Written Law, consisting of the five books of the Hebrew Bible that were given by G–d to Moses on Mount Sinai and include within them all of the biblical laws of Judaism. The Torah is also known as the Chumash, Pentateuch, or Five Books of Moses and is referred to by non-Jews as the "Old Testament." The Torah is a scroll made from *kosher* animal parchment, with the entire text of the Five Books of Moses written on it.

Tzitzit – tassels that hang down from the four corners of a rectangular garment worn under a shirt.

Yad – a Torah pointer.

Yeshiva – a religious school.

Yin jing – traditional Chinese for penis.

Zhongshan suit – a Chinese tunic suit. Named after Sun Yat-Sen. The four pockets on the front of the jacket represent the Four Virtues: politeness, justice, honesty and a sense of shame. The five buttons down the center represent the five branches of government and three cuff buttons stand for Sun's Three Principles of the People: Nationalism, Democracy, and the People's Livelihood.

Acknowledgments

I am grateful to Fran Morris Rosman and her husband Richard Rosman, the directors of the Ella Fitzgerald Foundation. Frannie gave me the opportunity to experience the joy, as an adult, of reading Torah at my *b'nai mitzvah.*

Thank you to Cantor Nathan Lam and Rabbi Ron Stern and Stephen S. Wise Temple, for introducing me to the little Shanghai Torah.

To my mother-in-law, Joyce Sitzer, my first editor and my comma queen. I'm grateful for your love and support. Thank you for championing this project.

To Gina Goldstone, who read an early draft and whose notes are valued and appreciated. Thank you for throwing your passion for the Jews of Shanghai into this story.

To Jimmy Huston, my publisher, thank you for the hours you have dedicated to this book; editing, proofreading, and publishing. The best compliment you gave me is, "Now you are an author."

To my script-writing partner, Lynn Mills, thank you for your passion and dedication to our projects. You have taught me to never give up, no matter how long it takes to realize a dream. I cherish our friendship. Thank you for proof-reading this book.

To Sharon Silverman, we have traveled many long roads in our lives and careers. I am grateful that you are by my side. You are a funny and caring port in a storm. You never got tired of me saying, "I'm working on my novel."

Thank you to my father, Melvin S. Spears, my beacon of wisdom.

To my son, Jordan Sitzer, you are my inspiration and overwhelming love.

To my brother, Eric Spears, your accomplishments inspire me to keep going.

To my brother-in-law, Michael Sitzer, for your loving care of me during challenging times.

****

To my husband, Charlie Sitzer, you are my heart, soul, and safe place. I love you.

About the Author

This is the first novel by Briana London, who began her writing career developing stories and scripts for Disney and United Artists. Over the years, her scripts have won many writing awards.

A graduate of the UCLA Film School, Briana is a two-time Emmy nominated film editor and won the ACE Eddie award for best episodic editing. Her credits include many popular episodic TV shows.

She lives in Los Angeles with her husband, son, two dogs, and a horse.